WHEN BOY BECOMES MAN

The wind rustled and something stirred in the brush. The stallion's head was up, nostrils flared. Suddenly, angrily, he pawed the earth.

In the brush, the grizzly called Three-Paws peered through the leaves. Deep in his chest, he gave a growl. He crept forward . . . one step . . . another.

Hardy's heart was pounding and his mouth was dry with fear. He backed toward the tree. "Betty Sue," he whispered hoarsely, "climb up. Climb to that big limb above your head."

Hardy stood with his back to the tree and notched an arrow. Old Three-Paws thrust his huge head from the brush and stared at the horse. The stallion blew shrilly, then reared on his hind legs, his front legs pawing.

And then Old Three-Paws charged.

Bantam Books by Louis L'Amour
Ask your bookseller for the books you have missed

BENDIGO SHAFTER
BORDEN CHANTRY
BRIONNE
THE BROKEN GUN
BUCKSKIN RUN
THE BURNING HILLS
THE CALIFORNIOS
CALLAGHEN
CATLOW
CHANCY
THE CHEROKEE TRAIL
COMSTOCK LODE
CONAGHER
DARK CANYON
DOWN THE LONG HILLS
THE EMPTY LAND
FAIR BLOWS THE WIND
FALLON
THE FERGUSON RIFLE
THE FIRST FAST DRAW
FLINT
GUNS OF THE TIMBER-
    LAND
HANGING WOMAN CREEK
THE HIGH GRADERS
HIGH LONESOME
HOW THE WEST WAS WON
THE IRON MARSHAL
THE KEY-LOCK MAN
KID RODELO
KILLOE
KILRONE
KIOWA TRAIL
THE MAN CALLED NOON
THE MAN FROM
    SKIBBEREEN
MATAGORDA
MILO TALON
THE MOUNTAIN
    VALLEY WAR
NORTH TO THE RAILS
OVER ON THE DRY SIDE
THE PROVING TRAIL
THE QUICK AND THE
    DEAD

RADIGAN
REILLY'S LUCK
THE RIDER OF LOST
    CREEK
RIVERS WEST
THE SHADOW RIDERS
SHALAKO
SHOWDOWN AT
    YELLOW BUTTE
SILVER CANYON
SITKA
THE STRONG SHALL LIVE
TAGGART
TUCKER
UNDER THE SWEET-
    WATER RIM
WAR PARTY
WESTWARD THE TIDE
WHERE THE LONG GRASS
    BLOWS
YONDERING

Sackett Titles by
Louis L'Amour

1. SACKETT'S LAND
2. TO THE FAR BLUE
    MOUNTAINS
3. THE DAYBREAKERS
4. SACKETT
5. LANDO
6. MOJAVE CROSSING
7. THE SACKETT BRAND
8. THE LONELY MEN
9. TREASURE MOUNTAIN
10. MUSTANG MAN
11. GALLOWAY
12. THE SKY-LINERS
13. THE MAN FROM THE
    BROKEN HILLS
14. RIDE THE DARK TRAIL
15. THE WARRIOR'S PATH
16. LONELY ON THE
    MOUNTAIN

DOWN THE LONG HILLS

LOUIS L'AMOUR

BANTAM BOOKS

TORONTO · NEW YORK · LONDON · SYDNEY

DOWN THE LONG HILLS

A Bantam Book / January 1968

2nd printing .... March 1968	4th printing ... February 1970
3rd printing ...... July 1969	5th printing ...... May 1970

New Bantam edition / April 1971

2nd printing ... March 1968	12th printing ..... April 1977
3rd printing . December 1971	13th printing .. January 1978
4th printing ..... July 1972	14th printing ..... July 1978
5th printing ... March 1973	15th printing ... August 1978
6th printing . November 1973	16th printing .... March 1979
7th printing . December 1973	17th printing . November 1979
8th printing ... August 1974	18th printing ..... May 1980
9th printing . September 1975	19th printing ..... June 1981
10th printing . November 1975	20th printing .... July 1982
11th printing ... January 1977	21st printing .. February 1983

*Photograph of Louis L'Amour
by John Hamilton—Globe Photos, Inc.*

ISBN 0-553-23377-7

Published simultaneously in the United States and Canada

PRINTED IN THE UNITED STATES OF AMERICA

H   30 29 28 27 26 25 24 23 22 21

To Jody and Jonna,
to Beau and Angélique,
each of whom contributed
something to this book

DOWN THE LONG HILLS

1

When Hardy Collins woke up, Big Red was gone. Hardy had picketed the stallion himself, and with sudden guilt he remembered that in his hurry to return to the supper fire he had struck the picket-pin only a couple of sharp blows.

He knew the horse was gone because from where he lay he could have seen its outline against the sky. He lay still for a minute or two, his heart pounding, frightened by what had happened.

Red embers remained of the cooking fire. . . . A coyote talked to the moon. In the wagon above him Mrs. Andy stirred in her sleep.

It was his fault that Big Red was gone. Mr. Andy was forever telling Hardy that he was old enough to accept responsibility; and aside from seeing his pa at the end of the trip there was nothing Hardy wanted more than to be considered responsible by Mr. Andy.

When folks crossed the plains together everybody had to do his or her part. Even Betty Sue, who was just past three, collected buffalo chips with her ma.

Careful to make no sound, Hardy eased from under the blankets and tugged on his boots. He knew by the stars that day was not far off, but he might find the stallion and get it back before anybody realized he was gone. And Hardy had a good idea where to look.

He was especially quiet because of Betty Sue, who tagged after him wherever he went. If she

1

woke up now she would ask questions. That was the trouble with women, Hardy decided; they just asked too many darned fool questions.

First, he got his canteen. Mr. Andy had warned him that a western man should never be without a canteen of water; and out where his pa lived water was a scarce thing, so it was better to learn that lesson now.

His hunting knife he always carried with him, because that mountain man who had stopped by for supper and a yarning time had said that if you gave an Indian or a mountain man a knife he'd make out anywhere, no matter what.

The circle of wagons was on a low hill with good visibility in all directions, and it was only a little more than a mile to the place where Hardy expected to find Big Red.

There was a seep back there with green grass all around, the best grass they'd seen in days, and when the wagons made camp for the night they had picketed the stock on that grass. When Hardy had gone out to bring him in, Big Red was of no mind to leave, and it would be like him to go back.

Out away from the wagons it did not seem so dark. He had walked almost a third of the way when he heard a rustle behind him and, scared, he turned sharply around. It was Betty Sue.

"You turn right around and go back," Hardy said. "What would your ma say if she knew you were out this time of night?"

"She wouldn't mind if I was with you."

"You go on back," he repeated. "I've got to find Big Red."

"I want to go with you."

She would surely get lost, Hardy reflected, if he made her go back now. Or she might even try to circle around and get ahead of him. It wouldn't be the first time she'd done that. "All right," he said. "But you'll have to be still. There might be Indians around."

She trudged along beside him, and after a while he admitted to himself that he was glad of her company. Not that he was scared—he had said that about Indians just to keep Betty Sue quiet. Mr. Andy and the men all agreed there were no Indians around this time of year.

There was a faint suggestion of gray in the eastern sky when they reached the coulee and found the big chestnut cropping grass. He looked at them, ears pricked, and then started toward them, dragging his picket-pin behind him. But when he was almost to them he stopped and his head and ears went up, his nostrils flaring as he listened into the night.

"You're sure spooky, Red," Hardy said. He picked up the picket-rope. "And you sure caused a sight of trouble, walkin' off like that. Suppose we'd gone off and left you? Then what would you do?"

Big Red was a stallion, but he was also a pet. Hardy had sat on his back when he was just four and the stallion was a frisky two-year-old. He was still skittish around strangers, and at times he could be mean. Especially, he hated anybody fussing around his tail. He would kick like a mule even if Mr. Andy tried to take the cockle-burrs out of it.

Hardy had cared for Big Red since he was a colt, and it was Hardy who fed him carrots and turnips, and took him to water. Big Red knew who his friend was, and had known it all his born days.

The trouble now was that Hardy was too short to climb to his back without help, for Big Red stood a shade over seventeen hands. Hardy could boost Betty Sue up, but he couldn't make it himself. Otherwise they could have ridden back to camp.

"Hardy . . . there's plums!" Betty Sue exclaimed.

Exasperated, Hardy looked around at her. "Plums! Everything is plums to you! Those aren't plums, they're blackberries."

Betty Sue was picking them and cramming them into her mouth with a cheerful disregard for names.

In the distance there was a popping sound like a
far-off breaking of branches, and Hardy glanced at
the sky.

It was too late now to get back undiscovered.
But if they took back a hatful of blackberries Mr.
Andy might be less likely to be angry.

Hardy thought he heard an animal cry, or a
baby. He listened, but heard nothing more, so he
went back to picking berries, eating about every
third one himself.

When his hat was full they started back, with
Betty Sue sitting up on the horse, hands and mouth
stained with berry juice. One thing you could say
for Betty Sue. She would do what she was told,
without making a big argument. A sight better than
most grown-up women . . . always arguing a man.
Even Mrs. Andy. She couldn't do anything without
making a lot of talk about it. Fussed more than a
jaybird over a garden snake.

They climbed out of the coulee to within a couple of hundred yards of the wagons. He could see
the smoke of the cook fires . . . that was an awful lot
of smoke!

All of a sudden he was scared. That was a lot
more smoke than he had ever seen, even that time
when somebody dropped some hot coals and started
a grass fire inside the wagon circle. He thought he
heard a sound of running horses, but when they
topped out on the next rise there was only the
smoke and what might have been dust.

The first thing he noticed was that the white
wagon-covers were missing. Of course, not many of
them were white any more, but out on the prairie
they looked white, and you could see them from
miles off, like a string of clouds floating close to the
ground. And there was no moving around and hook-
ing up, as there should have been at this hour.
When he had first seen the smoke he had dropped
back by Big Red and taken Betty Sue's hand.

Now his grip unconsciously tightened and Betty Sue cried out in protest.

Big Red stopped abruptly. His eyes looked wild, and he was smelling something he didn't like. Quickly, Hardy reached up and took Betty Sue from the saddle. Night after night before starting west he had listened to stories of Indian attacks and what had to be done about them. Squires, the mountain man who had stopped at their supper fire to eat and talk, had warned them, too.

Hardy had listened to too much such talk not to realize now what had happened. He drove the picket-pin into the ground and took Betty Sue by the shoulders. "You sit down," he told her. "I've got to go up there. You move one inch and I won't take you anywhere ever again."

She looked at him soberly. "I want mama," she said.

"You just set there. Set right there."

He trudged off alone, making slow time up the long slope of the hill. His heart was pounding heavily, and there was a lump in his throat he could not swallow.

There had been only twelve wagons in the train, but starting late in the season they believed they could make it through without trouble. The war party that had attacked them had been a small one, outnumbered almost two to one by the men of the wagon train, and the attack had been a surprise to both parties.

The Comanches, ranging far north of their usual haunts, were riding fast for home. They came upon the wagons unexpectedly in the first light of dawn. The guard had been stoking the fire for breakfast when the arrow struck him. Two others died in their sleep from arrows, and then the Indians swept through the small camp, knifing and killing.

There had been a brief flurry of shots when Mr. Andy reached his rifle and made a desperate at-

tempt to defend his wife. They died together, un-
aware that Hardy and Betty Sue were not with
them.

Hardy stopped outside the ring of burned and
half-burned wagons, gripped by a feeling he had
never known before. He had never seen death, and
now it was all around him, in this strange guise.
The stripped, scalped body of Mr. Andy did not
look at all like the man . . . nor did any of the
others look like the people Hardy had known. The
wagons had been hastily looted and set afire, the
bodies stripped and left as they had fallen.

Avoiding them, and embarrassed by their naked-
ness, Hardy searched quickly through the camp. He
would need weapons and food. There were no
weapons, of course—the Indians would have taken
those first. He did find some scattered cans of
fruit and meat, and some cans with the labels
burned off. Evidently the Indians had no acquaint-
ance with canned goods. He gathered up the cans
in an old burlap sack.

Some flour was there, but he had no idea how to
use it, and left it behind. Hurriedly, he left the
wagons and went back down the hill to Betty
Sue and Big Red.

Hardy Collins was seven years old, and he had
never been alone before . . . not like this. He
knew where the North Star was, and he knew the
sun came up in the east and went down in the
west. At home he had done chores around the
farm, had run and played in the wooded hills
with other boys, and for the last two winters he had
kept a trap-line down along the creek. He did not
know much more about the world except that pa
was out west.

He did not know how to tell Betty Sue about what
had happened, or whether she would understand if
he told her.

He dropped on his knees beside her. "We have
to go on alone," he said. "Indians came, and our

folks all had to go west. We have to go meet them."

It was a lie, and he did not want to lie, but he did not know what to tell Betty Sue, and he did not want her to cry. Nor did he believe that she knew what "dead" meant. The only thing he could think of was to go ahead now, and quickly. The Indians might come back, or the smoke might attract other Indians.

"Betty Sue," he repeated, "we've got to go."

She looked at him doubtfully. "I want my mama."

"We have to sneak away. Everybody ran from the Indians."

"Are we going to run away, too?"

"Uh-huh. We have to hide from the Indians."

She stared at him, round-eyed. "Is it like a game?"

"It's like hide-and-seek," he said, "only we have to run a long way before we can hide."

"All right," she said.

He boosted her to the stallion's back. It was all he could do to get her up there, but he pushed and she scrambled and the big horse stood patiently.

There was no way for him to get up on the horse. There were no rocks close by for him to stand on, no places where he might get the horse lower down than himself, and so scramble into the saddle. Taking the picket-rope, he led the horse and they started westward.

They were all alone. Ahead of them and all around them there was nothing but prairie and sky. There were no clouds this morning, and there was no dust. Neither was there a tree, a shrub, or anything taller than the stiff brown grass on which they walked.

The prairie was flat or gently rolling, with occasional long brown hills, tawny as the flank of a sleeping lion. There was almost no indication of distance, for there were no landmarks.

When they had gone on for what seemed a long time, and when the sun was high in the sky, Betty Sue began to whimper, so Hardy helped her down and they sat together on the ground and ate the rest of the blackberries. Then each of them took a careful drink from the canteen.

Betty Sue's eyes seemed to have grown larger and rounder. "Hardy," she asked, "will mama be very far off?"

"We won't see her today," he said.

When they started on Betty Sue walked beside him, as she had many times when he had gone to the fields to carry a lunch to Mr. Andy. When she grew tired he lifted her again to Big Red's back.

At last they came to a high place, and the long brown land lay before them in all its endless distance, miles upon miles of vast prairie, with nothing to be seen on it anywhere. And then, searching the land again, he did see something—between distant hills a smudge of blue, edged by green.

They started on, and Hardy no longer thought of the wagon train nor of the people who lay dead back there. Always before wherever he had walked, there had been the lights of home or at least a campfire waiting for him. There had been a good meal, and a bed at last. Now there was nothing like that; only somewhere far off, pa was expecting him, and in the meantime he was responsible for Betty Sue and for Big Red.

The sun was gone and the wind of evening was stirring the grass when they came at last to the slough in its shallow valley. At the water's edge the cattails were six feet tall and more. They found a place among a thick clump of willows where a trickle of water ran from some rocks down to the slough, and there they drank. The grass was good, and Hardy picketed Big Red carefully, talking to the horse all the while. Betty Sue was very quiet.

Once when the wind suddenly stirred the rushes Hardy turned around sharply, suddenly frightened, and Betty Sue looked as if she were about to cry.

"It's nothing. It is just the wind," he said.

He gathered cattails and dead grass and made a bed for them. After that he opened one of the cans with his hunting knife just as Mr. Andy used to do, and they both ate. It was some kind of meat, and it tasted good.

"Now you've got to wash your hands and face before you go to sleep," he said.

"All right," the little girl said meekly.

At the water's edge they both washed, and the water was cold and felt good on their skin after the long day of traveling. When they came back Betty Sue lay down on the cattails and Hardy covered her with his coat.

He sat down nearby, the knife in his hand. He had no idea what kind of wild animals he might have to fight but he would be ready. There were wolves, for he had seen them from the wagon train, and there were coyotes. In the creek bottoms sometimes there were cougars or bears, he knew.

The light faded and the stars came out. Wind ruffled the darkening steel of the water. He sat silent, listening to the comforting sound of Big Red tugging at the grass and munching it.

Vaguely, he recalled Mr. Andy saying it would take about a month to reach Fort Bridger where his father was to meet them, but that was with good luck and the wagons. How long would it take Betty Sue and himself, when he must walk?

It grew cold, and he was very tired. He lay down close to Betty Sue and wished the coat were big enough to cover them both. The stars looked like lamps in far-off houses.

A long time after he had fallen asleep he woke with a start. He heard the stallion breathing heavily, and he lay still, listening. Somewhere not far off he heard water splash and the sound of an animal as it drank. Lifting himself cautiously to one elbow, he peered through the branches toward the water's edge. A great black bulk showed there, and he waited, half-frightened. Then the big head lifted, drops trickled from its muzzle, and he saw it was a bull buffalo, and a large one.

It drank again, then moved away downwind of them, and when Big Red resumed eating Hardy lay back and went to sleep again.

When day broke gray over the hills, a gray shot with vivid streaks of widening crimson, he wanted a fire, but he feared it might bring Indians upon them. So he lay still, looking up at the sky, and thinking. They had been going west, and there was nothing for it but to keep on. With every step they were coming closer to pa.

He was used to walking on the farm and in the woods, and with the wagon train all of them had walked up the long hills to make it easier on the wagon stock. Of course, the wagons had always been there to crawl into when he was tired, but now there were no wagons, and he couldn't even get up on old Red.

Sooner or later he would find a big rock or a bank of earth from which he could scramble to Red's back, and after that he would always try to find places to stop where he could get up on the stallion's back again. Too bad pa had always insisted on roaching the stallion's mane, or he might have laid hold on it to help himself up.

Betty Sue slept without moving. Hardy knew they should be traveling on with the first light, but she needed the rest, so he got up quietly and took the stallion to water, within sight of camp. The horse drank while Hardy drank at the spring, and he refilled his canteen. When they walked back, Betty Sue was awake, but she didn't ask for her mama, or for anything else.

He opened another can and they ate, and drank cold water again from the spring. The sun was al-

ready high when they moved out. He looked
around for something to use to climb on the horse's
back, but there was nothing—not an old tree trunk,
the side of a buffalo wallow, or anything.

The country was less flat now, stretching away in
a series of long, graceful rolls of gentle hills. He
knew he should keep to low ground because of
Indians, but he wanted to keep a lookout for
another wagon train, or something.

He had not stayed with the wagon trail. He had
a feeling Indians might be watching it, so he stayed
over the slope when he could, but whenever he
topped out on a rise to scan the trail he could see
the ruts left by the wagons rolling west. As they
went along, a couple of times he found wild onions,
but Betty Sue refused to try them.

The day grew hot, and the brown hills were
dusty. Betty Sue whimpered a little, and he was
afraid she might cry, but she did not. He plodded
on, putting one foot ahead of the other at an even
pace, trying to forget how far he must go, and how
short a distance they had come.

As he walked he tried to remember all that pa
had taught him about getting along by himself, and
he tried to recall everything he had heard Bill
Squires say. There had been others, too, whom he
had heard talking of traveling west, of Indians, and
of hunting.

Once, far off, he glimpsed a herd of antelope,
but they disappeared among the dancing heat
waves. Again, and not so far away, he saw three
buffalo moving; they paused when they saw the
big red horse and the two children.

They were stragglers from the great herds that
had moved south weeks before. Men on the wagons
had talked of the wide track they made in passing. The big wolves had gone with them, following
the herd to pull down those too weak to keep up.
It was the way, Mr. Bill Squires said, that nature
had of weeding out the weak to keep the breed

strong, for the wolves could only kill the weak or the old.

Hardy took to watching Big Red, for he remembered something else Bill Squires had said: that a man riding in western country should watch his horse, for it was likely to see or smell trouble before a man could. But in all directions the vast plain was empty.

He studied the country, watched the movements of animals and the flight of birds. These could maybe tell you if somebody was near, or if there was danger of other kinds.

The sun slid toward the horizon and Hardy saw no place to stop. He plodded on, desperate in his weariness and the sense of responsibility that hung over him. When the last red was fading from the sky, Big Red began to tug at the lead rope, pulling off toward the south. Knowing the stallion might smell water, Hardy walked in that direction, with the stallion almost leading him. And then he saw the trees.

At first it appeared to be only a long shadow in the bottom of a shallow valley, but as they drew nearer the shadow became willows and cottonwoods, and there was the bed of a winding stream. No more than a dozen feet wide and scarcely that many inches deep, the water was cold and clear, and there was grass for Big Red and a place to hide.

He helped Betty Sue down and led the horse to water. There at the stream's edge his heart almost stopped. In the sand right at the water's edge was a moccasin track.

Filling the canteen with water without stepping off the rock, he hurried back and hid the stallion in a small clearing deep among the willows. The area was not large, but it gave the horse a bit of grazing and room to roll if he wished . . . and he wished.

Having made a bed for Betty Sue, Hardy then

opened another can. They were eating it when he saw something growing among the brush, something dark and about as thick as a stubby banana. Gleefully, he plucked it from the branch. "Pawpaws!" he exclaimed. "There's pawpaws!"

"I don't like pawpaws," Betty Sue said quietly.

"I didn't either, one time. Now I like them. You try one."

The fruit was almost four inches long and an inch and a half thick, greenish-yellow when he saw it close up. Searching the bushes, he found half a dozen more. Suddenly they tasted good, better than he remembered. Betty Sue ate hers quickly, then took another.

Excited as he was at finding the pawpaws, he kept remembering that moccasin track. He was not much of a judge of the age of tracks, but this one must be fresh. The edges of the track had not crumbled the least bit, and there were no marks of insects crossing it. That track had certainly been made that day, and probably within the last hour or two.

Though the moccasin track stayed in his mind, another thought was that he wanted a fire. There was something mighty comforting about a fire. That was what pa always said, and it must be so, because after ma died pa spent a lot of time just looking into the fire. It was then he started talking about going west.

Not that he wasn't doing well. Pa was a hard worker, and Hardy had heard folks talk of him, saying he was a man who would always do well. Mr. Andy had said it more than once. "You just watch that Scott Collins," he would say; "there's a man who is going to make tracks in the land."

A fire would have been a comfort now, especially for Betty Sue, but when he looked over at her she was already fast asleep on the grass, a half-eaten pawpaw in her hand. He covered her with his

coat and curled up close to her, and looked up at
the stars.

Where was pa now? How long would it be before
he knew what had happened to the wagons?

It would be a month before the wagons were
due. Why, he and Betty Sue might even get there
before pa realized the wagons were not coming!
Suddenly Hardy hoped so . . . no use pa to worry
more. He had been hard hurt when ma died.

Hardy had started following pa into the field
when he was not more than two, toddling and
falling, but watching and listening, too. By the
time he was a year older he was helping drop seed
potatoes, fetching and carrying for pa, and sitting
under the elms with pa while he ate his noon
meal. Pa used to talk to him about his work, and
sometimes about his dreams too. Other times they
talked about birds, and ants, and animals. Pa
taught him to set snares and to stalk game, as well
as to build quick shelters in the woods from any
material at hand.

As there were only the two of them, he helped
his father with everything. He used to pick up the
big, flat chips his father cut from logs that he was
shaping into square beams with an adze and a
broadaxe. The big logs would be notched every
eight inches or so along the four sides, and then
with the broadaxe pa would flake off the big chips
between the notches until the log was shaped into a
square beam. Hardy liked gathering them, and
they made a grand fire.

He had always gone to the woods with his father
when he went to search for herbs and nuts, or to
select the logs for the cutting. He could even help
with hoisting the beams into place when they
were ready to build the house. Using oxen, ropes,
and a greased log over which the ropes could
slide, the huge logs could be lifted into place.

At night they would sit by the fire making nails,
heating the long nail-rod, sharpening it to a point

with hammer blows, then indenting it at the proper length and breaking off the nail.

When not making nails, they wove baskets from reed fibers to make containers for grain and vegetables. Pa was so good at this that he often traded his baskets for food or other things he wanted to have.

When they were sitting together of an evening, pa would tell Hardy stories of his own boyhood in his native Ireland, and how he had been apprenticed to a millwright when he was ten years old. At fifteen he had been tall and strong enough to be swept up by a press gang and taken off to sea, but after a year of that he left his ship in New Orleans and went up the Mississippi and the Ohio, and then over the mountains to New York. From there he had gone to sea again, this time as a ship's carpenter, and after the voyage he worked around New York, and had gone to New Hampshire, where he met ma.

After ma died they had gone west, as far as Wisconsin, but even there pa was still restless. He wanted a larger place, in more open country where he could raise horses. At his home in Ireland there had been fine saddle stock all around, and it was such horses he intended to raise.

Once when pa went off to market he left Hardy alone for two whole days and nights. Somebody had to stay and care for the stock, and keep the crows out of the corn. When pa returned Mr. Andy was with him, and he took up land close by.

Pa had been listening to stories about California; but it had not been the gold that took him off across the plains, but the attraction of a good climate and a place to ranch horses. He had been gone for a year when he sent for Mr. Andy to come west and bring Hardy.

Suddenly Hardy found himself awake, scarcely aware he had slept. The sky was faintly gray. Easing away from Betty Sue's side, he got Big Red and led him to water, then went back to camp and picketed the big horse again.

Among the trees and brush he found some straight shafts for arrows, and a good piece for the bow. His father had taught him how the Indians made their bows and arrows, and he had often hunted rabbits and squirrels with them. Working kept him from thinking now how hungry he was, and how hungry Betty Sue must be. He ate another of the pawpaws as he worked.

He was just finishing the bow when he heard the horses coming. Big Red heard them first and his ears went up and his nostrils fluttered as if he was going to whinny. Hardy caught the lead rope and whispered, "No! No!" Big Red was silent, but he was very curious.

Watching under the willows, Hardy saw three Indians with feathers in their hair. All were naked to the waist, and one had a quarter of an antelope on his saddle. They drew up about thirty yards downstream, and Hardy could hear the low murmur of their voices. He noticed that they were not painted, and they carried no scalps.

One of the Indians dropped from his pony and lay down to drink. As he started to rise he hesitated, then stood up. When he came to his full height he looked upstream, and for a long moment seemed to be looking right into Hardy's eyes. The boy knew he could not be seen, but he held very still and prayed that neither Betty Sue nor Big Red would make a sound. After a long, long minute, the Indian looked away.

Soon all three rode off together, with the others, but even as they left, the one Indian turned and looked back. Hardy held very still until they had gone, and then he woke up Betty Sue.

He knew that they had to get away from there. They must leave right away. For that big Indian, he felt sure, was going to come back.

2

Bill Squires squatted on his heels, his back to the pole corral. "About the fourteenth, it was. I come down the left fork and seen a fresh wagon trail stretched out across country.

"It was late to find a wagon train, but I went down the trail after them, figuring on some talk, an' borrying coffee offen them. Then I was right curious to see what they meant, travelin' so close to snow time."

Bill Squires spat and rolled his quid into the other cheek. "Mornin' of the sixteenth I come up with them." He glanced at Scott Collins. "Yes, I recall the boy. He was sure enough there, and Andy Powell's girl a-taggin' after him every step. Good boy. Bright, an' chock full of questions about Injuns an' sech."

"You knew Powell?"

"Hell, yes! I should say. His pa an' me was friends back in Pennsylvania when Andy was born. I knowed Andy, all right. Ever' time I went back home I'd see him. Wasn't often I went home, of course, but time to time. He told me about the boy and the horse."

He glanced sharply at Collins. "No Injun better see that stallion. He'd give an arm for him. I'm not speakin' of 'Paches now. They ride a horse half to death, then eat them. I'm speakin' of the Cheyennes, Sioux, Kiowas, and them. They know horseflesh."

Scott Collins sat very still, feeling sick and empty

17

inside. He had been hoping and praying that something had happened to keep the boy from starting west. He did not know what could have happened, but he had been hoping for something, for anything.

"Two, three days later I cut Injun sign. Comanches, an' a sight too far north for them. Weren't more than nine or ten of them, but they were drivin' a dozen shod horses an' a few head of cattle, so they'd been raidin'.'"

He paused, spat, and said, "Now look at it. Them Comanches were a long ways from any settlement, and no Comanche is any hand to drive cows, not when he's far from his home country. It figured they had raided somebody close by and hadn't had a chance to eat the beef.

"It had to be them wagons, so I taken off. The way I saw it, the Indians had probably killed them all, yet some of those folks might be stranded back there with no stock an' winter a-comin' on. The men with the wagons outnumbered the Comanches, so they might have out-fit 'em.

"No such luck. Looked to me like the Indians come up on 'em about sunup. Nobody had a chance. A body could see the way the bodies lay what happened. No ca'tridge shells anywhere but by Andy Powell's gun. I figure he got a few shots . . . nobody else did."

"What about the youngsters?"

Scott Collins had to force the question, but he did not want to hear the answer.

Squires glanced at Collins sympathetically. "Now, I'm not one to give a man useless hope. I buried all the bodies I found, an' there was no boy among them the size of yours, nor that girl of Andy's either."

Nobody said anything for several minutes, then Scott Collins got out his pipe and stuffed it with tobacco, forcing the fear and grief from his mind and fighting to think logically. Now, if ever, he must do that.

"No young un would have a chance to get away," Darrow said. "Not out on bald prairie, that away. Comanches must have packed 'em off."

Squires chewed thoughtfully. "Doubt it," he said finally. "Them Comanches was travelin' fast. They didn't even keep a woman to take along. This was a quick raid, hit-an'-run like, with them Comanches few in number an' a long way from home.

"You see, this here is Cheyenne country, rightly speakin'. Oh, there's other Injuns about, time to time, but a small war party wouldn't want to waste around an' risk runnin' into the Cheyennes or Pawnees."

He paused, then said, "Collins, I hesitate to give hope to a man when there's mighty little reason for it, but I figure those youngsters got away, somehow."

After a moment he added, "Two youngsters, out on the prairie that way . . ." He let the words trail off.

Scott was thinking, trying to put himself into Hardy's place. Oddly enough, it gave him confidence. The boy was a serious youngster, and he was pretty canny about wild country. Maybe he was being foolish, just trying to give himself hope, but despite his struggle to be cautious, he had a feeling Hardy was alive.

"If you didn't find their bodies, and if you think the Comanches didn't carry them off, then they must be back there, somewhere."

"Now, I don't know. How long could those youngsters make it, out there with no food, no beddin', an' no way to get on? Still," Squires added, "one thing has worried me ever since I left that burned-out wagon train. What become of the big stallion? I studied that Comanche sign, an' believe me, I could point out the track of ever' horse in that outfit this minute, but there sure was no track of the stallion amongst them."

"Hardy would get away with that horse if he could manage it," Scott Collins said. "They grew up together. That stallion followed him like a puppy dog from the time it was a bitty colt."

He knocked out his pipe and got to his feet. "Squires, I'm going back. If those youngsters are alive, I've got to find them, and if they aren't, I'll find their bodies and give them decent burial."

Bill Squires looked out from under thick brows. "Comin' on to winter out there, boy. The weather was nice enough when I rode through there, but she's due to break any day now." He paused, "Scott, you got to face it. If those youngsters got away, an' I'm thinkin' they did, they're dead by now. There just ain't no way they could live out there."

Collins shrugged into his coat and picked up his rifle. "That boy of mine worked right alongside me since he could walk. He's bright, and he's old for his years. He knows how to build snares and he's killed rabbits with a homemade bow and arrow . . . made them himself. I brought him up to care for himself.

"Another thing," he added, "if the boy is alive, he will be expecting me. As for Big Red, that stallion will outrun anything on the Great Plains. If those youngsters get up on that horse no Indian will ever lay hands on them."

"All right," Bill Squires got to his feet, "no two ways about it. We'll go have us a look."

"You're a couple of fools," Darrow grumbled. "Injuns killed those young uns, much as I hate to say it." He looked up at Collins. "No offense, Scott, but you got to look at it. If you go back there you'll get killed into the bargain."

"That boy's all I've got, Frank."

Darrow reluctantly got to his feet. "You're a couple of witless wonders; but Scott, I can't let you

go off into wild country alone with Squires. He'll
get you killed sure as shootin'."

The sky was gray, and a cold wind came down
from the Wind River Mountains. There was snow
on the peaks and the high timber, and the bunch
grass on the plains where the three men rode
looked brown and used up.

"You know the boy," Squires said, "so you'd best
be thinkin'. You put yourself in his place, try to recall whatever the boy knows, an' you figure out
what he's likely to do."

How to put yourself in the mind of a seven-
year-old with a tiny girl and a horse? If, in fact,
they were with him. That was the worst of it, they
did not know.

Yet there were things he did know. For one,
Hardy was stubbornly persistent, and for a boy of
his years he had been alone a good bit. And of one
thing he was sure. Hardy would try to come west,
and unless something prevented he would hold
close to the trail.

He held himself tight against the fear that was
in him, the fear that grew until his heart throbbed
heavily and his knuckles grew white on the reins.

Hardy, his son . . . his boy . . . was out there
somewhere, in danger of his life. He was not out
there alone, either. He had a little girl, almost
a baby, to care for.

Squires must have guessed his thought. "Scott,"
the old mountain man said roughly, "you got to
forget what's happenin' out there. You got to think
just of how to find them. You got to live each day,
each hour, by itself. You think any other way and
you'll go crazy."

Scott Collins forced himself to think calmly. It
was plains country where the wagon train had been
attacked and burned, but not far west of there the
country broke up into gullies, rolling hills, and

some long valleys, with the mountains to the north of the trail, but close by. There were trees along the watercourses, and sometimes there were patches of trees along the ridges.

The year was dry and there would be little water, but the boy had listened well, Squires had said, and he might remember some of Squire's advice to the wagon-master on water holes. Yet he would have to beware of regular water holes because of the Indians.

One by one Collins added up Hardy's assets for survival. He knew a few words of Sioux and Chippewa—that came from living near Indians along the Wisconsin border. He also knew a little of the sign language. Occasionally Indians had stopped by the cabin and Scott always fed them, and sometimes they had come by to leave a quarter of venison. The year of the big fire when much of the forest burned after a thunderstorm, and the game ran away to the south, Scott had kept a dozen Indians alive with gifts of food . . . even sometimes when it meant they went short themselves.

"The wagons were three days out of Laramie Crossin' when the Indians hit 'em, an' those youngsters aren't goin' to make the time they should, havin' to hunt grub." Squires rolled his tobacco to the other cheek. "We got a good many miles to go before we come up with 'em."

"You traveled fast," Scott said, "having horses cached for you, and all, but how long do you figure those youngsters have been on their own?"

"I taken a message east," Squires said, "an I had horses hid out for me. I swapped horses three times. I figure those youngsters been out a week or so . . . not less'n six days."

It was a long time. How could they eat? With no rifle, they would get little game . . . although with a bow and arrow Hardy could likely get a rabbit or a ground squirrel. Maybe even a sage hen.

The three men rode hard and they stopped seldom, and as they moved their eyes studied the ground and the hills around. They were still far from where they might find tracks of the children, but Scott was fearful of passing them.

Near the mountains they saw deer, and several times came across antelope tracks. Once they came upon a herd of elk, and another time they saw wild horses. They left the trail to look at them, but there was no red stallion among them.

"No Injuns yet," Frank Darrow said, "an' that's a blessing."

"They don't like this country at this time of year any more'n we do," Squires said. "Come winter, they head for the hills an' hole up in some nice valley where there's wood and such."

"Bill," Collins asked, "what would Indians do if they caught the youngsters?"

"Your guess is as good as mine. I've known 'em to smash their skulls against a tree or rock, but also I've known 'em to take youngsters in and care for 'em. Among their own, Indians treat their youngsters mighty good . . . better than most white men. With captives now, it's another story. You just can't tell."

After a moment, he added, "I'd say the younger they are the better their chances."

They pushed on until their horses were gaunt and lagged upon the trail. The time came when Squires said, "Scott, we've got to rest these ponies, else we'll find outselves afoot."

"Bill, they can't be far off now. We've got to push on."

"If you kill these horses you're likely never to find 'em. Think, man!"

"Creek up ahead if I remember rightly," Darrow commented. "There'll be grass an' water an' fuel. I say we lay up a day, rest the horses, and scout around a mite. Meanwhile we can sort of

take stock, consider the country up ahead, an' try
to figure where we stand."

It was good advice, and Scott knew it. And the
camp they made was a good one, sheltered from
the wind and the eyes of any passing Indian, with
the branches of trees to thin out the smoke from
their fire.

Dusk had come by the time they had stripped
the gear from their horses and staked them out on
grass. Scott Collins walked up the low hill beyond
the camp and stood listening into the night. Big
Red could really move if they gave him his head,
and he might have carried them this far. He was
a fine horse and he loved that boy.

But the night wind was cold. Would Hardy have
a coat? And what about Andy Powell's little girl?
If she had just up and followed Hardy off, she
would be lightly dressed, in no shape for a cold
fall in Wyoming.

For more than an hour he stayed on the knoll,
straining his ears for any sound, seeking to identify
each one, hoping with all that was in him for the
sound of Big Red's hoofs, or the faint cry of a child.

Bill Squires came up to join him. "Scott, this
ain't doin' you no good. Come down an' eat. Get
some rest. Frank's throwed together some grub, an'
you sure look peaked."

"They're out there somewhere, Bill . . . we've got
to find them."

"If they're alive, we'll find them."

The dancing fire brought no comfort, but the
food was good, and the strong black coffee helped
to lift their spirits a little.

"We'd better stand watch," Squires suggested.
"Me an' Frank will stand the first two. Get yourself some sleep."

And Scott Collins did sleep, and while he slept
he dreamed of a great red stallion and two children, who rode on and on through endless nights of
cold.

3

After the fourth day Betty Sue asked no more about her mother, nor did she cry at all. Her face became thin, her eyes unnaturally large. She clung to Hardy, so close he found it difficult to picket the stallion or hunt for food or fuel.

They had come to the crossing of Pole Creek, but they found it dry in both directions. There was grass, very good grass, and despite the lack of water Hardy stopped long enough to let Big Red fill his belly. And then, for the first time, he found a place where he could mount the horse.

There might have been other such places, but from the reverse slopes where they walked, the country along the river, seen in occasional glimpses through gaps among the low hills, looked as dangerous as it did inviting.

He mounted the horse from a bank of the creek, and at once they moved away at a good clip. Big Red was restive and eager to go. He had been worried all day, Hardy could see it in his manner; and the horse did not like the feel of the cool wind coming out of the north.

On this day they ate the last of their small store of food, a can of beans. Betty Sue ate hungrily, then looked longingly at what still remained of Hardy's, so he gave it to her, hungry though he was.

He thought of the big Indian. Though there had been no sign of him, Hardy was not reassured. The Indian had probably said nothing to the others, wanting their scalps for himself, and wanting Big

Red. It could be he was pursuing them even now.

During the course of the day they crossed and recrossed the creek bed, once finding a pool of water. There was water in the canteen, so they did not drink, Hardy not liking the look of the water, but the stallion drank, and gratefully.

The sky was an unbroken gray when they started on again, and the bluffs were covered with dead pines. The day was bleak and cold. Big Red moved out anxiously, eager to be going. Hardy studied their back trail from time to time, but saw nothing disturbing.

Several times he saw rabbits and tried shots at them, but the third one he saw he did not try for, since there was no way to get back on the horse after retrieving the arrow if he missed.

When he at last found a place to camp, he was hungry and tired. Too tired to be scared, but not too tired to be cautious. The camp he made was under dead pines, below a bluff covered with them. There was only a trickle of water in the creek, and the grass was dry and brown. They found nothing to eat, and although he set some snares he had small hopes for them. It was a cold, miserable, unhappy night, and toward morning it began to rain. Nothing was in the snares, and there was nothing to do but go on.

Big Red wanted to trot, so he gave the stallion his head and let him go. Today they stayed with the main trail, for Hardy knew that Indians will not ride in the rain unless circumstances demand it.

The rain slanted across the gray sky like a steel mesh, and under the hoofs of Big Red the trail grew slippery, but the horse kept on untiringly. Huddled on his back, holding Betty Sue before him, Hardy lost all track of time. Finally the big horse slowed to a walk, but he plodded on. Around them the land grew rougher.

Now the ridges were crested with trees, and

along the watercourses there were some big old cottonwoods. Hardy straightened up in the saddle and peered around him. He must find shelter, and somehow get some food. Betty Sue was too quiet, and it frightened him.

Hardy was learning to see. Back in the woods one always had to be alert, he knew, but there the range was narrower. Even when he was riding the wagon seat, the view was always somewhat obscured by the other wagons, by riders or dust. Now, riding high on Big Red, he could see further, and from hearing the mountain man talk, he had learned something about looking and seeing.

All people look, but few really see; and they can rarely give details of any place they have passed —its appearance or what might be found there. Hardy was looking out for trouble, but now he was looking for food too, for something—anything —they could eat.

Just before dark the rain stopped, but the sky remained overcast. They had only a brief time in which to find shelter before night came, but shelter was no longer so difficult to come by, for there were frequent deadfalls, hollows under the banks of a stream, or thick clumps of trees.

Presently he found a huge cottonwood that had fallen, its top resting on the bank of a stream. Its boughs were still hung with dead brown leaves. Alongside it was a green slope leading down to the stream, and on this slope he staked Big Red, after watering him and rubbing him down with handfuls of grass. Betty Sue sat in a woebegone little huddle near the tree, watching him.

Hardy crawled in under the tree and broke branches until he had shaped a hollow into which they could crawl. The broken branches he then wove in among those stretching out to the sides, to improve their shelter. He gathered the longer grass and weeds to make a mat several inches thick to cover the ground.

Under a slab of rock that had fallen across two boulders he found a place big enough to hide Big Red, where he could lie down. Hardy tugged and sweated, getting some stones out of the sand so Red could rest easier.

He was cold and tired, and shivered in his wet shirt, but it was Betty Sue who really troubled him. She sat so silent, asking none of her usual interminable questions, only staring with big, frightened eyes. He suddenly realized that she reminded him of a woman back in Wisconsin, a neighbor whose husband had died. She had sat still like that, talking to no one, and then one day they found her dead. Hardy gave a little shudder as he thought of this.

Yet, he reassured himself, they had come a good way today, and every step brought them closer to pa; by now pa must be looking for them. On that one thing his faith did not waver. Pa would come, and he must care for Betty Sue and Big Red until he did come.

He planned to set five snares, but by the time he had found places to set two he was too cold and tired to go on with the others. Returning to their shelter, he lay down beside Betty Sue and huddled close to her. During the night it began to rain again.

The soft patter on the leaves above them was strangely comforting. He felt Betty Sue stir beside him and he spoke to her, making his tone confident. "Pa will be coming soon. He said he would meet us."

"I'm hungry," Betty Sue said.

It was the first thing she had said all that day, and he caught at it quickly. "So'm I. Tomorrow I'll get out an' hunt. Don't you worry, Betty Sue— I'll find something."

But even as he spoke, he knew his chances would be slim. Wild life did not like to move when the weather was wet; aside from the discomfort, the dampness caused them to leave more scent behind.

Animals knew better than to stir around in wet weather.

Suddenly Hardy decided: if it was raining tomorrow, or even if it wasn't, they would stay right where they were. They had water, there was good grass on the slope for Big Red, and the shelter was keeping off the rain—well, almost. Even as he thought they were snug and dry, a big drop fell down the back of his neck.

There might be fish in the stream. Maybe nothing but suckers, but he had eaten suckers before this and they were good enough. Not like the pickerel and pike from Wisconsin, but still pretty good eating when a man was hungry. And he had seen some bird tracks, like those of a prairie chicken, only larger. Maybe one of those sage hens he'd heard the mountain man speak of. . . . His thoughts trailed off, and he slept.

He had forgotten all about that Indian.

Several times the damp cold awakened him, and once the coat had fallen off. He covered Betty Sue and himself again, and lay awake several minutes listening to the rain.

Fort Bridger was west of here, somewhere beyond South Pass, and maybe somebody would be hunting out of that fort, and would find them. Hardy thought of the warm kitchen smells back home, and of the gaiety and laughter around the campfires on the way west.

Suddenly a chilling fear swept over him. Suppose something had happened to pa? Suppose he wasn't coming at all?

The distance seemed so far. A month, Mr. Andy had said, a month by wagon train without having to walk as he had, without searching for food. Three more weeks and a bit over. Could Betty Sue keep going that long?

He sat up and clasped his arms around his knees. He daren't think of that. He just had to keep going. What was it pa used to say? "Give me a stayer every time. I like a man or a horse who just gets in there and keeps on going."

But how could they keep going? Betty Sue was already so thin it frightened him to look at her.

As soon as it was light he had to get out and rustle, rain or no rain. So far he had only looked for food when they traveled, or when they had stopped for the night. He had not deliberately taken time out to hunt for it.

Finally he lay down again and went to sleep, and the rain whispered him into a deeper, sounder sleep, all his tired, aching muscles relaxing slowly. The rain fell gently upon the brown grass, over the powdery dust, over the trees and the rocks. It fell where the horse had walked, and slowly the tracks disappeared, fading out bit by bit under the caressing touch of the rain.

The big Indian, Ashawakie, was curious, as any wild thing is curious. Ashawakie had been trained from childhood to observe, and when he saw a little riled-up water floating by he knew something close upstream had disturbed it. When he looked that way he thought he caught the sheen of sunlight on a chestnut or sorrel flank. He had also thought he glimpsed a momentary shadow upon the waters, but he might be wrong. He said nothing to the others with him, for if there was a chance to count coups, he wanted it first; and if there was a horse to steal, he wanted the first chance at it.

Horses meant wealth to him, for an Indian was judged by the number of horses he had. Coups meant pride among the maidens, meant boasting by the campfire. Ashawakie was a great warrior, he had proven it many times; but he was a warrior who liked to work alone. Now, when he could find an excuse, he left the others and circled back.

He discovered the tracks quickly enough, but was puzzled by them. The tracks of the horse were large, but those of the people—two of them —were small. Young ones? *Alone?*

He dismissed it as unlikely. . . . The Little People? He felt a shiver of superstitious dread. The Old Ones had left stories behind of the Little People, and he wanted nothing to do with *them.* Anyway, they were supposed to have disappeared long ago into a cleft in the mountain far away in the northern Big Horns.

Of the two people whose tracks he had found, he rarely saw the tracks of the much smaller one.

The sign left by the horse excited him. The stride was long and even, the stride of a big, smooth-traveling horse that could hold its pace hour after hour. He wanted that horse, Little People or no.

But he soon felt assured that they were not the Little People. They must be children of the White-Eyes, and they were alone. They had built fires rarely. He found no scraps of food, no bones. Only at first did he find a tin can.

Ashawakie could read sign, and like any Indian worth his salt, he deduced a good deal from what he saw. These were children alone, hurrying westward, and they had no food.

He found where snares had been set, but there was no blood and no hair, no feathers. They had caught nothing. But the Little Warrior, as Ashawakie came to think of him, had removed the snares before he left, wanting none of the Forest People to be trapped and die after he left.

Ashawakie was a Cheyenne. He did not make war upon children, but he was curious; and after a while, he was faintly admiring. The Little Warrior was cunning. He chose his camps well. He hid his horse. Before leaving each camp, he tried to remove all sign of his presence. He only rode in the trail after the rain began, when a few hours, or even minutes, would wipe out all trace of his passing.

Interested, Ashawakie followed. He had no idea

what he would do when he came up to them. He
wanted the horse. The children would be a nui-
sance. Still, the boy would make a warrior, and he
was young enough to be raised as one of them.

Hardy awakened to find it was daylight, and the
rain was still falling. No game was likely to be
about in the rain, but he must look—he might come
across something.

The air was gray and heavy, and the tree above
him would scatter the smoke, so he took a chance
and built a fire, then rustled wood. The fire
would be a comfort for Betty Sue while he was
gone.

"You've got to stay here with Red," he told her.
"I've got to find something to eat, and I can't do
it with you following after. You stay close to the
fire and keep warm."

Whether it was the warmth of the shelter, cou-
pled with her own waning strength, Hardy did not
know. Perhaps it was the fire and the presence
of Big Red, but at any rate Betty Sue was willing
to stay behind, and agreed not to stir, no matter
how long he was gone.

Taking his bowstring from his pocket where he
kept it coiled and dry, he strung his bow. He had
only three arrows, but he hoped they would be
enough. He took them and stepped out into the
rain, keeping the bow close to his body to shield
it from the wet.

There was a huge, lightning-blasted cottonwood
near the shelter, and he chose that for his land-
mark. Instead of walking swiftly away, he walked
off a short distance, looked back, then walked a
slow half-circle past the shelter to see it from every
point. He knew how even the most familiar things
can seem different when looked at from a different
angle.

Then he began to hunt. Hollow trees, clumps of
brush—anywhere an animal might hide. The trees
here extended only a few hundred yards beyond

the stream, but in some places the distance nar-
rowed down to only a few feet, but there was
brush along the stream and on some of the hill-
sides near the water.

Once he started a rabbit, but it was gone before
he could notch an arrow. He would have to try
for them at sundown, when they were more apt to
sit still and look around; even if startled they would
usually stop at the edge of a hiding place to look
back.

He had been gone for almost an hour and was
about to turn back when he saw a clump of bushes
about four feet high . . . hazelnuts!

He went to them quickly. Many of the nuts had
fallen, but he found dozens still clinging to the
branches and he picked his hat full.

By the time he went back to the shelter the rain
had stopped and there were breaks in the clouds.
Betty Sue was there waiting for him; she seemed
to have hardly moved. Huddled over the fire, they
cracked open the hazelnuts with a small rock and
ate them.

After that Hardy put out the fire and scattered
earth over it to smother any remaining coals. Then,
putting Betty Sue on Red's back, he led the horse
down into the stream. On the bank he found a
place where he could climb to the stallion's back,
and he walked the horse upstream until near the
hazelnut bushes.

The sun shone bright, and it felt good on his
back and shoulders. He had almost forgotten what
it meant not to be wet, cold, and hungry. When
they reached the hazelnuts he rode out of the
stream, found a place where he would be able to
remount, and picketed Red on the hillside grass.
Then he proceeded to pick nuts until his hat was
full again, and the front of his shirt too. By that
time there were few nuts left.

He mounted again, and walked the horse along

a winding trail, made by buffalo, no doubt, that followed the stream along the opposite side from that he had traveled thus far. In case the Indian was behind him the rain might have wiped out Hardy's tracks, leaving no sign for the Indian to find. By crossing the stream, wading in it for a short time, and then following the opposite bank, he might lose the Indian completely.

The day was warm and clear, but they made slow time because the track led along a steep slope above the river. Trees on the banks masked their movements. About midday they halted and Hardy staked out the horse on good grass; he and Betty Sue ate more of the nuts. He was about to start on again when he saw the chokecherries. Only a few were left, but the taste of them, even though they puckered the mouth, was somehow refreshing after the nuts.

After a while they went on, and the sun was pleasant after the chilling rain. It had only taken a few of the nuts to fill them up, and he carried those that were left inside his shirt.

Presently Betty Sue fell asleep, and he cradled her head against him until his arm was so stiff he could scarcely move it, but he did not want to wake her. When she slept, she was at least not afraid.

He was trying to think. What was it his pa had said so often? "Remember, son, the only thing that makes a man able to get along in this world is his brain. A man doesn't have the claws a bear has, nor the strength of a bull. He doesn't have the nose of a wolf, nor the wings of a hawk, but he has a brain. You're going to get along in this world as long as you use it."

He couldn't count on it that pa would be hunting for him. Scarey as it was even to think of it, he knew he had to think of what he would do if pa didn't come.

They had to keep on to Fort Bridger. There

were people there, and there he and Betty Sue
would be safe. There were womenfolks who would
tend to her, and it was a place where he could
sleep without being scared what he'd wake up to.

But Fort Bridger was a long way ahead, and the
country was getting higher. Last night it had been
almost cold enough for frost, and any night it might
really freeze. It had snowed this early, too, a time
or two.

Maybe he had lost that Indian who was trailing
them—or who he thought was trailing them. But
maybe the Indian was coming on, wanting their
scalps, and wanting Big Red. Hardy wanted to believe they would see no more of him, but pa had
always taught him to be foresighted.

"Try to foresee the worst things that could happen," pa said, "and plan for them. Figure out what
you would do beforehand. Chances are, they'll
never happen; but if you plan ahead, you're ready."

Well, all right, he would think of those things
later. Now he had two things he had to be thinking
of right off. They were going to need more food,
and some way to fix something warm to eat or
drink. Somehow he had to get some meat. And he
had to figure out some way of cooking something
if he caught it.

Also, they were going to need something warm to
wear. He was cold all the time, except when right
in the sun, and Betty Sue shivered, even under his
coat. He tried not to think of how far they had to
go, or how short a distance they had come so far.

Meanwhile, he had to look for a camp, a hidden
place where he could see around without being
seen, and a place where he could get back on the
horse.

Ashawakie was eager to find that big horse. He
had lost the trail because of the rain, but he rode
on. Shrewdly, he was paying little attention to trail

sign . . . instead, he was trying to foresee what the Little Warrior would do.

That was how he found the crudely made shelter under the dead cottonwood.

4

Frank Darrow swung his horse around and studied the tracks. "Injun pony," he said. "Scott, you've got to face it. Any chance we had to find those youngsters was washed away by that rain. Look for yourself . . . there ain't any tracks to be seen. Not even antelope tracks."

Collins indicated the pony tracks. "That Indian was going somewhere. If he left tracks, we can find Hardy's tracks."

"If he's alive to make any." Darrow rested his hands on the pommel. "Scott, I ain't sayin' I wouldn't feel the same, was I in your boots, but you've got to see reason.

"That youngster is only seven years old, and he's up against a fix no grown man would like to face. He's out in the wilderness with no grub, no weapon that we know of, an' he's got him a girl kid to care for. You say he knows how to get along, but this here is Injun country an' he's got him a horse any Injun would give his eyeteeth for.

"You talk about gettin' along. This here country this time of year has mighty little game. There'll be cold winds blowin' down across this flat like the mill-tails of hell in no time at all. The Injuns an' the game know that, so they head for sheltered places in the hills. Your kid ain't got a chance."

Scott Collins nodded his head. "Frank, you go along back and I'll not hold it against you. I know winter is coming on and you've got stock to feed and work to do. You've got wood to cut and lay

37

by before cold weather sets in. I've got to keep
looking, and you know why? Because I know that
boy.

"He's followed me to the field and the woods
ever since he was knee-high to a grasshopper, and
he's questioned me up one side and down the
other. We've hunted plants in the woods and fields,
and sold them to folks for medicine. We've hunted
them for grub. He's helped me with the planting,
and he's got a mighty keen sense of responsibility.

"He's known some Indians. He's played with their
youngsters, and he's hunted with them. I know my
boy; and young as he is, he'd take a lot of killing,
believe me.

"And that isn't all. There's just the two of us
now, him and me. And he knows that I'll be hunting him. I'll be along the trail somewhere, and he'll
trust me to look, because he knows that's the way
I'm geared. Frank, it may take me a long time, but
I'll not stop hunting until I find that boy, or find
his body. You go along if you're of a mind to."

Darrow stared at him. "I never knew such a
pig-headed, stubborn fool in my life. All right, I'll
stay with you, but only for one reason. If that boy
is half as stubborn as you are, he's probably too
stubborn to quit or to die. Let's get to huntin'."

Bill Squires had been studying his chewing tobacco. Now he bit off a bite and tucked it into his
cheek. "If you two sidewinders would quit arguin'
long enough to think, you'd be askin' yourselves a
question."

They looked at him, and Squires took his time.
He got his jaws to working on the tobacco, and
was enjoying the suspense. "Yessir. If you two
would stop to think, you'd ask yourselves what that
Injun was doin' out here in the rain."

They stared at him, and he rolled the tobacco
in his jaws. "Now you look at that track. That there
Injun pony left that track sometime before the rain
quit. She's a fairly fresh track, edges not broken

down, yet there's a showin' of water in it, and there ain't goin' to be much seepage in that kind of clay.

"So what have you got? You got an Injun who's away to hell an' gone out in the open, ridin' through the drivin' rain . . . that's before he got to this point. An' no Injun is fool enough to do that—not unless he's close to his wickiup, he ain't.

"Now, we ain't close to no camp or we'd have seen sign before this. That Injun is ridin' alone through the rain, which no Injun is likely to do. So I got to ask myself why."

"You think he's following the youngsters?"

"Scott, an Injun would trail them kids through the worst storm you ever did see to get that stallion. This here's the first promise we've had."

"It's a slim chance," Darrow agreed reluctantly. "Come to think of it, it *is* odd. An Injun would find himself a place to hole up until the storm was gone."

"We got nothin' else," Squires said, "so let's try her on for size."

It was a slow, painstaking task to work out the trail. The Indian had held to hard surfaces when he could find them, and occasionally his tracks had been washed out by rivulets. Once they rode half a mile on trust because a belated rush of water down a stream bed had washed the sand free of any tracks after the Indian's passing. Sure enough, further on, after an hour of scattering out and searching, they picked up a track.

It was the Indian who led them to the shelter under the dead cottonwood.

They reached it at the end of a long hard day, and made their own camp there. Bill Squires studied it with interest. "He's a canny lad, that one," he said admiringly. "He had himself a nice camp fixed up here, and one nobody was likely to find."

"That redskin found it," Darrow commented wryly. He indicated the fire. "He covered that up well. They've been eatin', too." With a stick he pushed several charred shells out of the fire. "Hazelnuts."

"Look here." Squires had found the impress of a tiny hand on the dirt beside the bed—just the outer edge of a palm, a smudge where the knuckles must have been, and the slight print left by the thumb. "He's got Andy Powell's girl with him, all right."

Hardy had left a small pile of wood neatly stacked against the bank on which the top of the tree rested, and they used it now for their own fire.

Frank Darrow fried bacon and made up some frying-pan bread and coffee. Bill Squires sat musing and smoking. He rarely smoked on the trail.

"We've got us some trouble," he said finally.

Darrow looked up, and Collins stopped shaving kindling for the morning fire.

"You've told me a lot about that boy," Squires said, "an' I can see a good deal around here. He knows that Injun is after him."

They waited, while the bacon sputtered in the pan and the smell of coffee filled the small shelter.

"It's more a feeling than anything else. But look at this place. He took pains to hide out. He wasn't just makin' himself a shelter—he tried to cover it up, too.

"He's got a knife. We've seen places he's used it, but not around this camp. Nothing sticks out more'n a fresh-cut tree or limb with the white wood showin'. Well, did you see any around here? This boy must be dead-tired, he must be scared, but he's usin' that little head of his all the time. I'd lay a bet that if a body took time you'd find scattered places where he cut firewood all through the trees yonder, but you'd have to hunt for them. I doubt if he'd be that careful unless he suspicioned somebody was huntin' him . . . somebody other than his pa."

"Why do you say we're in trouble?" Collins asked.

"The kid will hide his tracks," Darrow answered, "sure as shootin'. He figures to meet you comin' up the trail, but that Injun is behind him, an' he ain't goin' to leave him nothing if he can help it. That means he ain't leavin' anything for us, neither."

Over their meal they studied and discussed every possibility they could think of. Hardy Collins would not want to leave the trail where he knew his father might be searching, yet he might be forced to do just that.

Scott felt sure about what his son would do, and on that score the two mountain men agreed with him. He was sure that on leaving camp Hardy would take to the water so as to leave no tracks— but where would he go then?"

"We got to find where he found them nuts," Squires said. "If there was more, he'd go back after them."

Scott Collins could not sleep. He lay awake a long time thinking of his son out there in the cold and dark. By day Collins could keep a bold face before the other men, and by day he was confident of what his son would do, or try to do; but at night when he lay down in the darkness he could only think of how frail even a sturdy seven-year-old can be.

Hardy had grown up to an outdoor life, of course —in fact, he knew no other life. Many a time he and his father had camped in the woods together; they had gone off hunting, each in his own direction, and had left signs for each other to indicate the way they had gone. They had often rustled meals for themselves from small game and wild herbs. Nevertheless, he was only a small boy, caring for a smaller girl. . . . Finally Collins drifted off into sleep.

He had been awake for a minute or two, hearing the low sound of voices outside, before he realized it was early morning. When he opened his eyes he found a fire going, smelled the coffee, and heard Darrow speaking.

"In lookin' for this youngster, Bill, we'd better not forget that Injun. He'd like to notch his stick

for our scalps, no doubt, an' we'd best keep a
weather eye open for him."

Scott Collins sat up. "Wonder one of you
wouldn't give me a call. I'm overdue for some coffee."

They both ducked their heads and came in
through the small opening. "You looked plumb
tuckered out, so we let you sleep," Bill said. He
was smoking his pipe. "Whilst Frank was fixing
grub, I took a look around. There's a clump of
hazelnuts right across the stream an' up a ways.
Plenty of sign around there. The boy must have
loaded up on them, judgin' by the fresh pickin'
sign he left."

"He's not starving, anyway," Scott said.

There was very little conversation. When Scott
had finished eating, the three men, with Bill
Squires leading, went down to the stream, and they
followed it, eying the banks carefully. They came
to the hazelnut patch, and went on. From time to
time they saw sign left by the Indian.

The tracks were now several days old, but they
did not dare increase their pace for fear they would
lose the vague trail—and sometimes there was
hardly a trail at all.

Late that afternoon, Scott Collins drew up, studying the tracks of the Indian. "Does it seem to you,
Bill," he said, "that this Indian spends a lot of time
checking out the way those youngsters get along?
Every time he comes on a place where they've
stopped, he leaves enough tracks for four or five."

Squires chuckled. "He's curious. They've got him
puzzled, Scott, an' it seems to me he's real interested. He wants to see how they're getting on,
an' what they have to eat."

"Hardy knows a good deal about getting along
in the outdoors, if he'll just use his head."

"He's got his troubles," Darrow put in. "There's
a lot he can't fix to eat because he's got no dish or

pot. For somebody travelin' light, I'd say he's gettin' along all right."

"How far are we behind him now?" Scott asked.

"Two, three days. Maybe four. . . . He travels
awful slow at times, an' I figure he didn't make
over four, five miles the first day out. Maybe less
the next day. But when he can get up on that horse
they usually make good time."

They were in camp when Collins suddenly
looked around at the others. "I'm afraid he'll quit
the trail."

"I've been thinkin' on that, too," Squires agreed.
"The way I see it, it's his only chance to get
away from that Injun. Might not do it even then,
for the Injun is good on readin' sign, but if he
could pick the right time he might ride north an'
get into the deeper woods, cut across until he hits
the foothills of the Wind River Range, an' then cut
down for Bridger. The boy might do just that.
He's thinkin', all he can."

"I wish they were dressed warmer," Scott said.

"Yeah . . . so do I."

Ashawakie was thinking about the cold, too, but
not in the same way. Several times he was sure he
would catch the Little Warrior, but each time they
had slipped away somehow. In their camps, they
kept the fire small, as an Indian does, and huddled
close to it, but the wind was blowing cold off the
mountains where there was snow. At any time the
streams might begin to freeze along the edges,
and the Little Warrior and the small girl would be
cold.

But Ashawakie was not thinking of them with
pity. That they might suffer from the cold aroused
no response in him. He was simply aware of the
fact, curious as to what they might do, and he
knew that he must calculate upon it in searching
out their camps.

He had known few white men, and no white women or children. Many of his people had known them, and some had spoken of them with favor; but most Cheyennes had only known the white man to fight him or to steal his horses, though the Cheyennes placed less emphasis on the virtue of stealing horses than did the Comanches.

Ashawakie was no more concerned with the feelings of the children than he would be with those of wolf cubs. The horse was what he wanted, but he was much interested in the way the Little Warrior faced his problems.

The Indian did not, as yet, realize that he, too, was followed. As did all Indians, he watched his back trail, but the three white men were still too far behind him for him to know about it. Had he guessed they were following him, he might have made a desperate effort to catch the children, kill them, and take the horse. He was now too far from his own wickiup to think of taking them back as prisoners.

But Ashawakie had more to think of than the children and the horse, for he was nearing the place of one of his greatest tests. It had happened three years ago, when he met the bear.

The Cheyenne was thirty-five years old and a strong warrior now, but he admitted to himself that when he met the bear he had known fear—for the first and only time.

The bear was a grizzly, and Ashawakie had come upon him unexpectedly. He had seen at once that the grizzly was in no good frame of mind. Some animals, like some men, are born with a chip on their shoulder, and the grizzly had a chip on his. He saw Ashawakie on the narrow trail, and Ashawakie whipped up his rifle and fired.

The bullet struck and the grizzly lunged, snarling. There was no chance to reload, and the Indian jammed the rifle into the bear's jaws and grabbed his hunting knife. The bear slapped the rifle from his jaws; Ashawakie got one swipe at an upraised paw with his knife, and then he was knocked off the trail.

Luckily, he fell clear, struck a clump of bushes, and dropped flat on his face in the sand beside the stream. The wind was knocked out of him, or he might have moved. As it was, he had just got his breath when he heard the enraged bear coming down the slope some sixty yards away.

Snuffling, and making an angry rumbling sound, the animal nosed around among the bushes and rocks for some time before the pain of his wounds took him away. There had been nothing to guide him, for in falling, Ashawakie had left no trail, and the bear's search was futile.

Ashawakie looked around now and muttered to himself, remembering the happening. It was his closest brush with death, and he recalled the episode and the area with distaste. Was it an omen, that he had been led back here by the children?

Were they children, or were they, after all, the Little People? Had they brought him back again to this place where he had known fear? To the place of the bear?

5

Until now, Hardy had lived in a state of apprehension, fearing the dangers of the trail less than he feared his inability to cope with them. But now, suddenly, he found himself confident. They had been on the trail for several days, and they had survived.

He was up on Big Red and the stallion was moving along at a pleasant gait. Betty Sue was sleeping peacefully, and for the first time she was not whimpering in her sleep. But above all, he felt that he was thinking well about their situation.

It was the fish that began it. Hardy had crossed the stream twice during the last half-mile, and then had re-entered it and traveled a quarter of a mile upstream in the water.

There are few trails that, given time, cannot be worked out by a good tracker, and Hardy had small hope of losing the Indian. All he could do was play for time; and perhaps he could gain as much as an hour—maybe several hours.

It was while riding in the water that he saw the fish, and for the first time he began to realize how much his worry had kept him from making the most of the country.

Back home he had often watched the Indian boys making fish traps of branches and reeds; in fact, he had helped them, and had caught fish by that method. Here he was, going hungry with a stream close by that was filled with fish.

His arm was aching from supporting Betty Sue's

head, but his mind was busy with the problem. To make a fish trap he would need a little time . . . he could make one, with good luck, in an hour or less. He could set it at night, and perhaps find fish in the morning. His bad luck was that he had to keep moving. . . .

Or did he?

Suppose he left the trail? By now the Indian would be sure he was headed west, as most white men were, and was keeping to the trail. What if he selected some not too obvious spot and left the trail entirely? Suppose he took to the hills and camped beside some small stream until he could catch a good meal or two, perhaps even enough fish to smoke a few for the days ahead?

He could broil the fish over a fire, or in the coals. As far as that went, he could make a dish out of bark, as his father had taught him. There were plants around that could be cooked with meat or fish . . . he just had not been thinking.

The air was fresh and cool, the stream rustled along over the rocks, and occasionally wind stirred in the trees. When the wind came down off the snowfields on top of the mountains, it was chill. Several times, topping out on small rises among the trees, he had looked back. So far he had not seen the Indian once, but he felt sure he was back there.

The trouble with leaving the trail was that he might miss his father, who he still felt must be searching for him. But his father was a man who used his head, and he knew how Hardy thought. Of course, in the past there had been those signs they left for each other, signs to indicate a change of direction, or to show when the trail was abandoned. Undoubtedly any sign he left for his father the Indian would see, too. The usual way to leave sign was with rocks: one or two rocks piled on top of another, with a rock beside the pile to in-

dicate direction, or a broken branch to point the
way.

From among the trees Hardy looked ahead
and saw where, a few hundred yards off, a smaller
stream flowed into the river from the south. It
was just what he wanted.

Descending the bank, he found a good place to
get into the water, and then rode along upstream.
The water was rarely more than two feet deep,
and was running swiftly. Riding along until he was
opposite the inflowing stream, Hardy went on upstream a short distance farther, and then came up
out of the water and, doubling back through the
trees, rode a little way toward the hills.

After he had gone a short distance, he returned
to the bank of the larger stream at the spot where
the smaller one entered it, and placed a broken
branch in a bush beside the trail, the butt end of
it pointing in the direction he had taken. There
was a chance, since Hardy had not used such a
method before, that the Indian might miss its sig-
nificance. His father, he was sure, would be looking
for such signs as they had used for each other,
and this one was the most frequent.

That night Hardy and Sue camped by a small
stream near a grove of willows, and Hardy set
to work to make his fish trap. First, he gathered
a number of thin willow withes and tied them all
together at one end with another, thinner withe.
Then he made several hoops, graduated in size,
and pushed the smallest hoop as far down toward
the tied end as possible, and tied it to the willow
withes. He placed the other hoops, each somewhat
larger than the next, within the cone of willow,
tying each in place. When he had the trap ready
for use, he put it in the stream and returned to
their camp.

Remembering the fish trap had jogged his
memory about other things, and he thought of the
arrowhead, or *wapatoo*, a water plant growing in

ponds and slow-moving streams. The tuberous roots could be boiled like potatoes, or roasted in hot ashes. He remembered that there had been two seasons when the potato crop failed, and he and his father had eaten the *wapatoo* instead. The Indians used to find them while wading and would pick them with their toes from under the muddy water. Hardy wished he could find some now.

Foraging around through the brush the children found a few more nuts, which they ate as they searched, and also some chokecherries. It was not enough to satisfy their appetites, but it did help.

The night was cold. The stars were clear and bright. The gleaming mountain peaks were crystal sharp against the sky.

When daylight came, his fish trap had three good-sized trout in it and, baked in coals, they tasted good. For the first time neither of them felt hungry.

The deep glen where they had taken refuge was reached by a narrow trail, long untraveled, to judge by its condition, except by wild game. They had found a spot concealed among great fallen trees, and although there was little grass, the stallion browsed off the low-growing plants and brush, and seemed content. During the day Hardy spitted several fish on sticks above the fire and smoked them as best he could, and while the fish smoked the children gathered serviceberries. It was then that Hardy found the track.

He had never seen a grizzly bear track before, but he knew it at once by the long claw marks made by the front feet. He had heard about these from Bill Squires.

The grizzly had apparently been gathering berries there, perhaps only the day before, and his tracks were all around. Hardy studied them with care, his scalp prickling as he thought that the bear might not be far away. Of course the grizzly might travel far in foraging for food—he might be miles away, even now. But the thought of the roasting nuts or fish . . . if the bear was anywhere nearby, the smell would attract him.

Later, Hardy found more tracks on the open trail, and he was puzzled by something. One of the forepaws, he decided, was curiously crippled, and mentally he began to call the grizzly Old Three-Paws.

It was already late on the second day in the glen when Hardy found the tracks. To leave now, with their fish still not thoroughly smoked, and to ride out and try to find another camp at this hour was more than he wanted to do.

"We'll stay," he said to Betty Sue, "but if you hear anything in the night, you touch me awake. But don't move, and don't speak."

She looked at him with big eyes. "Why?"

"Just do what I tell you," he said firmly.

"Why?"

He did not want to tell her, but it was better than having her asking questions. "I think there's a bear somewhere around," he said, "a big bear."

Suddenly he thought of Big Red. The small space in which he had picketed the stallion gave him too little room. It was no more than fifty yards across, and scarcely that wide. Not enough room to get away, nor enough to fight in, and no living creature he knew of could match a grizzly. And Hardy thought that, while a grizzly prefers nuts and berries or roots, he would not miss a chance to add red meat to his diet.

It was already dusk, but he made his decision—they would have to leave. They would have to go at once.

Hurriedly he began to get their few things together. He started toward Big Red, and the horse side-stepped nervously, keeping his head turned toward the forest. His ears were pricked, his eyes wide, his nostrils flaring.

"All right, Red," the boy said gently. "You let me put Betty Sue up. We're going to leave."

The stallion ducked his head a little, but his eyes stayed on the forest.

Old Three-Paws was coming on. He was a huge grizzly, a little past his prime, and he was cranky. Born with a streak of meanness, it had doubled and redoubled since the injury to his paw long before.

He had been on a long sweep around his territory, a sweep some twenty miles around, and he was coming back to that corner he much preferred. He was returning from an unsuccessful hunt, hungry and fierce.

The wind was from him and toward them, or he might have caught the man-smell then and turned aside. But as he drew nearer he caught tantalizing, unfamiliar odors mingled with familiar ones. He recognized the smell of horse—he had eaten horse once or twice—and he knew the smell of raw fish.

Old Three-Paws weighed about nine hundred pounds. He was not quite as quick as he used to be, but he was still quick, and he could crush the skull of an ox with one blow of his good paw. He feared nothing on earth, and earlier that day he had lumbered past a mountain lion. It spat and snarled, then darted past him on the narrow trail, turning to snarl after him. Old Three-Paws ignored the cat as something beneath his notice.

He was not far from the camp when he first smelled horse; then he got the smell of smoke, which he did not like, and that tantalizing smell of smoked fish, which was different from any smell he had ever encountered before.

Old Three-Paws stopped on the trail and lifted his nose inquisitively. He was not afraid, but he was curious. This was a narrow, secluded canyon. His own den, where he would soon be crawling in for

the winter, was only a short distance farther on.
He sniffed again, and growled deep in his chest.
Now there was, faintly, a tinge of man-smell on the
wind.

He left the trail and went down the slope toward
the water, pausing from time to time to sniff the
wind. He drank at the stream, stared into the
gathering dusk, for it was darker among the trees,
and then he turned again toward the smell. He
was hungry, and he wanted meat . . . and there
were, too, other possibilities of food where the man-
smell was. He had raided camps before this . . . and
gotten away with it   .

Three miles farther back on the trail, Ashawakie
had come upon the trail of his old enemy. With a
thrill of supersitious fear, he recognized the bear
track, then noted the crippled forepaw. He remembered his last, desperate swing with the knife, and
the paw streaming blood. That had been his final
glimpse of the red-eyed bear as it knocked him
sprawling over the cliff.

Ashawakie, descendant of generations of warriors
stood irresolute.

Only a little farther up the trail was the great
red horse . . . he had found hairs left in the bark
where the horse had scratched himself . . . and he
wanted that stallion. The children—if real children
they were—would be there too. . . . And the bear.

The tracks of the bear were fresh, made only a
short time before; and that bear had almost killed
him once. For months, although he told no one,
he was charged by a red-eyed bear in his dreams,
and he would wake up cold with sweat, seeing again
those slavering jaws, those gleaming teeth, and the
wrinkled, curled-back lips.

He checked his rifle, then the bow and arrows he
carried against the possibility of damage to the rifle.

Ashawakie had his own pride, a fierce pride in
his strength, and he had taken many scalps,

counted coups many times. He would ride on. But
the fear of the bear rode with him, that bear that
was, that must be, an evil spirit incarnate, a monster who lived only to destroy him. His fingers
strayed to his medicine bag, and touched it lightly.
He would need his medicine.

A wind moved the leaves ever so gently, and
Hardy's eyes grew round as he moved toward the
horse to lift Betty Sue to its back. The stallion side-
stepped quickly, moving away from the burden for
the first time. Hardy hesitated, wanting desperately to be away, yet aware that the stallion sensed
danger and wanted to be free to move.

He led Betty Sue to a large tree, and hoisted her
to a limb. "You sit still," he warned, "and don't
make a sound."

He got out his bow and his arrows. They were
pitiful weapons against the might of a grizzly, but
he had nothing else.

Again the wind rustled, and something stirred in
the brush. Crossing to the big horse, Hardy reached
up and unsnapped the picket-rope from the halter.
"There you go, Red, you do what you need to do,
and I'd not blame you if you run out of here."

The stallion's head was up, nostrils flared. Suddenly, angrily, he pawed the earth.

In the brush the grizzly peered through the
leaves, his red eyes blinking. Deep in his chest, he
gave a growl. He recognized the stallion for what he
was, or should have been, the leader of a herd.
He had met such creatures before, but usually they
fled, leading their mares away in a swift rush that
left Old Three-Paws far behind. Only when he was
about to attack a mare with a foal did the stallion
stand to fight; and there are few things more
terrible in battle than an infuriated mustang stallion.

Three-Paws took a slow step forward. The stallion

was a good twenty yards off, and the grizzly
wanted his first charge to be decisive. One blow of
his good paw and that stallion would be down with
a broken neck; but the grizzly knew from past experience that a fighting stallion was like a demon
unleashed, swift to dart in, to spring aside, to re-
treat.

Big Red was larger than any mustang stallion
Three-Paws had ever seen, but the grizzly was not
worried. He merely wanted to get it over with
quickly. He crept forward . . . one step . . . another.

Hardy's heart was pounding, and his mouth
was dry with fear. He backed toward the tree.
"Betty Sue," he whispered hoarsely, "climb up.
Climb to that big limb above your head."

Betty Sue was a good climber—she had always
been good at it ever since she first followed Hardy
into the forest. Now she got up and climbed easily
to the limb that was another four feet above the
ground.

Black bears can climb trees swiftly, and a young
grizzly will often climb. But a mature grizzly will
not, because of his weight. Hardy stood with his
back to the tree and notched an arrow.

Old Three-Paws thrust his huge head from the
brush and stared at the horse. The stallion blew
shrilly, then reared on his hind legs, his front legs
pawing.

And then Old Three-Paws charged.

6

The grizzly had expected with that juggernaut charge to smash the stallion back against the brush and trees, where the weight of the bear's body would carry the horse off balance long enough for teeth and claws to do their work.

The stallion leaped aside, pivoting on his forefeet and letting go with both iron-shod hoofs. The kick caught the bear on the shoulder and flank as he reached the end of his charge, and it was he who was knocked off balance, falling on his bad side.

He was up instantly, but not in time to escape the driving strike of the stallion's forefeet, smashing down for a kill. The bear moved, evading one hoof, but the other ripped a great gash in his shoulder.

Warily, as if realizing that until now he had been lucky, Big Red circled the bear. Three-Paws reared up on his hind legs, wanting to get in a blow with his forepaw that might break the stallion's neck or his leg. It was at this moment that Hardy chose to let fly with his first arrow.

It was not a particularly good arrow and it was not shot from a particularly good bow, but the distance was less than fifty feet and the white spot near the base of the grizzly's throat made a perfect target.

Hardy drew his bow to its utmost, and let go. The arrow shot true, striking the bear in the throat,

a bit to one side, but going in for more than half its
length.

The grizzly struck at the stinging in his throat,
then half-turned, staring toward his new enemy.
He caught sight of the boy near the bole of the tree,
and instantly he went for him. Hardy, his bow hung
over his shoulder, was already scrambling up the
tree when the bear glimpsed him. The branches
were low, for he had chosen the tree well, and
Betty Sue was already climbing higher to give him
room.

As the bear charged for the tree, the stallion
leaped in, great jaws agape, and slashed the bear
on the hindquarters. The grizzly wheeled, striking
a mighty blow that would have ripped the stallion
apart had it landed; as it was, it left a long thin
streak across one side that almost instantly began
to show blood.

Old Three-Paws was really angry now. He stood
there staring, shifting his eyes from the stallion to
the boy in the tree; but mostly he watched the
stallion as it moved back and forth in front of him,
well beyond reach, but within leaping distance if
the bear gave the stallion a chance.

A fighting stallion is an awesome creature, able
to rip with teeth, clamp with mighty jaws, kick
with the hind feet, or strike with the forefeet, yet
Hardy knew that Big Red was no match for the
grizzly, even a crippled grizzly such as this one
was.

But the grizzly had been badly hurt. The kick
had knocked the wind from him, his side hurt him
now, and there was bleeding from his shoulder and
rump, but it was the arrow in his throat that worried him most. He tried to get at it with his teeth,
but he could not. He heard the stallion start, and
waited with slavering jaws, the foam now mixed
with blood.

"Red!" Hardy yelled. "No!"

The stallion was beyond hearing, beyond caring.

Before him was his enemy, and he started forward, almost dancing, neck extended, lips curled back over his great teeth.

Ashawakie rested on one knee in the brush. He had seen only a little of the terrible fight, just a glimpse of it in the few seconds since his arrival; and the whole fight had not yet lasted a minute. Carefully, he lifted his rifle, watching for a good shot at the bear.

This was his old enemy. Here was his chance to destroy his fear. If this was a medicine bear, as he almost half-believed, his bullet would be useless; but if it was not, his old enemy would be destroyed, his fear gone forever.

Ashawakie took careful aim, the bear turned slightly, and Ashawakie eased back the hammer. In the stillness, as the stallion moved forward, cat-footed, the click of the hammer was loud, and it was a sound Old Three-Paws had heard before. He turned toward the sound, and Ashawakie's finger tightened . . . tightened . . . his eye held on the sight-picture. . . . Suddenly the rifle leaped in his hands, and the great bear, struck full in the chest, staggered back and went to all fours.

Hastily, the Indian started to reload.

Old Three-Paws heaved himself to try to rise up, but he only succeeded in falling back on his haunches.

Now, Hardy thought—if I could only get Big Red. If I could drop on his back, and get Betty Sue down from the tree, we could slip away.

He called again, this time more softly. "Red! Big Red, come here!"

The call reached the stallion and he hesitated, still wanting to attack, yet fearing the bear, knowing the danger that lay in the grizzly. Again he heard the call, more insistent now, and somehow the old habits of love and obedience fought down his fury, his instinctive lust to destroy lest he be destroyed.

Old Three-Paws was puzzled. He had come here to kill a horse, not such a creature of fury incarnate as this, nor had he expected to be assailed on every side. Again he tried to snap at the irritating thing thrust into his throat.

He started to growl, and coughed on the blood trickling down his throat. He heaved himself up, and started for the horse. Ashawakie, within his place of concealment, worked desperately to reload . . . the bear must be destroyed, the horse must be saved.

Big Red had almost started toward his master, but the movement of the bear stopped him. He knew he must not turn his attention from the monster. His only hope lay in swift movement, sudden strikes.

Three-Paws was moving toward Red, and Hardy raised his bow, drew back the arrow, and let fly. He missed.

One more arrow. He lifted the bow again . . . too late. Big Red, whistling shrilly, rushed at the bear. The grizzly reared up to strike, but the stallion dodged as if struck by a whip-lash, and slashed wickedly at the bear's rump and flank. Three-Paws tried to turn, but something was wrong with his side where those crushing hoofs had struck before. He began to turn, and the iron jaws of the stallion ripped him again. Then Three-Paws lunged, and his weight hurled the stallion from his feet, knocking him to his side on the grass. With a deep snarl of triumph, the bear lunged for the kill.

And the rifle spoke again.

The bullet smashed against the grizzly's skull, striking at an angle. The bullet did not penetrate, but the bear was stunned, half-crumpling, as if to his death, then suddenly he heaved himself up and threw himself into the brush where the shots had come from.

Hardy dropped from the tree so swiftly that he

ripped the hide from his arm and skinned one knee, tearing his pants. He ran to the stallion.

"Red! Red! Oh, Red!" He was sobbing in fear, but the big horse managed to get up, shook himself, and started to where the bear had gone. Leaping, Hardy caught him by the halter.

"Come!" he pleaded. "Red, please come!"

He led the horse to the tree, snapped the picket-rope again, and scrambling to a low limb, helped Betty Sue to Red's back. The big horse was trembling, partly from fury, partly from his fall, but he stood still at the boy's pleading voice, the voice he knew and loved so well. Hardy scrambled from the limb to his back. "Let's go! he whispered.

The stallion hesitated. They could hear the bear floundering in the brush, but there was no other sound. Reluctantly, the stallion let himself be turned away. Scrambling out of the hollow, Hardy found a dim trail and took it, then he deliberately headed back for the river.

He was nearing it when he saw a dim trail left by wagons—not many wagons, and long ago, but it was a trail and it was pointing westward. Red took it at a gallop, then slowed to a trot. Leaning over, Hardy could see the red streaks left by the bear's claws. Behind them there sounded another shot.

There was still light in the sky, and the crimson along the ridges was just fading, the higher clouds still flushed and pink above them. Hardy had no thought except to escape, and he rode swiftly. Once away from the scene of the fight, Big Red seemed eager enough to be going, and they made good time, crossing a shoulder of the mountain by a faint trail, and descending toward the river.

There they came upon an old wagon trail, and Hardy followed it, content to be headed west, or almost west.

He had no idea who had been shooting from the brush, but he suspected it was the Indian who had followed them. All he could think of was that they were getting away, leaving the grizzly behind. Now, for the first time, he was aware that he was really frightened. It came over him all of a sudden, and he clung, trembling, to the stallion's back.

After a while he felt better; the stars came out, and the big stallion moved on steadily, seemingly in no hurry to stop for the night. A light wind came down from the mountains, cool from the snows and fresh from the pines. Several times Hardy almost fell asleep, but the horse plodded on, regardless.

The trail turned slightly north, then still farther north, but Hardy was only half awake, and scarcely noticed. They came out of the trees into a valley of long meadows, streams, and scattered clumps of trees. And then, suddenly, the stallion stopped.

Hardy opened his eyes wide. Betty Sue was asleep in his arms, but the big horse, ears up, was staring ahead, and seemed to be scenting the air.

Hardy sat up tall and peered past Big Red's head. Some distance off, right down on the ground, there was a light . . . a fire!

A campfire . . .

Hardy's heart took a great leap . . . it must be pa! Pa had come hunting for them! He slapped his small heels against the stallion's side and started forward. But, the big horse hung back, seemingly reluctant to go on.

Could it be Indians?

Hardy rode more cautiously. Suddenly, somewhere ahead, a horse whinnied, and there was a flurry of movement near the fire.

Hardy walked the horse a little closer. He could see two saddles, some pack saddles, and a coffee-pot on the fire, and there was a smell of bacon. . . .

"Set right still," a voice said, "or I'm likely to fire. Now you jest walk that horse right up to the fire an' le's have a look at you."

Hardy tried to speak, but his throat was tight. He walked the horse forward, and suddenly he heard the voice say, "Hell, it's a couple of kids!"

"They come from somewhar," the other man said. "That means thar's folks about."

"Here? At this time of year?"

"Well, look at 'em."

One of the men was lean and somewhat stooped; he had a hard, angular face and small cruel eyes. He walked forward, looking at Big Red. "Jud," he exclaimed, "would you look at that horse now? Man's there's a *hoss!*"

"He belongs to my pa," Hardy managed to say.

"Well, mebbe. Whar is your pa, boy?"

"He's . . . he's back on the trail. He's hunting us."

The other man was shorter, barrel-chested. He walked slowly up to them, studying the stallion. "You mean he don't know whar you be? How'd that happen?"

Betty Sue wakened and was staring at the men, wide-eyed. She felt tense in Hardy's arms, as if frightened. Well, Hardy reflected, so was he. There was something about these men . . .

Hardy explained briefly how their wagons had been burned, how they had started on west. Once he started talking, he told them about the Indian, then about the grizzly.

"Aw, come off it!" The shorter man scoffed. "A grizzly'd kill you quicker'n scat. No horse can match up to a grizzly!"

"Red wasn't afraid. He fought him."

"Reckon he did, at that," the taller man said, "He got clawed along the ribs." The man reached a hand up for Red's bridle, and the stallion jerked his head away.

"Don't you pull away from me, damn you!" The tall man lifted a hand to strike Red, but the stallion swung away and Hardy said "Don't you dare strike my horse!"

"Take it easy, Cal," Jud said, more quietly. "You're likely to lose 'em all. I figure we better let those kids have some grub an' sort of study on this a mite."

"I don't like any horse actin' up with me. What he needs is a taste of the club."

"Cal's just a-talkin', boy. Now, why don't you two git down? We got us some grub here, an' in the mornin' we can sort of figure out what to do. Mebbe we can find your pa for you."

Hardy didn't like the looks or the sound of these men, and he wanted nothing so much as to ride away, but the two men were standing too close. One of them was all poised for just such a move, so though he didn't want to, Hardy slid to the ground. He would wait until the men were asleep, then they would slip away.

The man called Cal started to reach again for the bridle, but Red pulled back, eyes rolling. "Let me stake him out," Hardy said. "He knows me."

"You jest do that, youngster." Jud looked past him, shaking his head at Cal. "Your little sister, she can jest stay here with us. No use her wanderin' around in the dark, out yonder."

When he had picketed the stallion, Hardy went up to Red and rubbed him gently on the shoulder. "Looks to me as if I got us into trouble, Red. You be careful now. Maybe we can get away from them."

He walked tiredly back to the fire. Betty Sue was seated on a rock near the fire, her eyes big and staring.

Jud looked over at her. "Now how old would that one be, boy?"

"She's three," he said, "just past three."

"Don't seem reasonable," Cal offered, "you two out here alone like that. You say your pa is huntin' you? How d'you know that?"

"I just know it. That's the way pa is."

Cal chuckled. "Chances are he figures the Injuns killed you. He ain't huntin' you, boy."

"That's not true!" Hardy was near to tears. "He is so hunting us!"

Hardy ate some food while the two men talked, muttering together in low tones. Finally Jud brought them a blanket. "You two roll up in that. We'll have us a talk in the mornin'."

Cal glanced over at them. "An' don't do any wanderin' about camp. I got a mighty touchy way with a gun. I might mistake you for an Injun."

When they were covered up near the fire, Betty Sue whispered, "I don't like those men!"

"Ssh!" After a moment Hardy said, "I don't like them, either!" Then he added, his lips close to her ear, "Maybe we can slip off."

With the best intentions of staying awake, he fell sound asleep. He had been tired for such a long time, and now for the first time in days he was under a blanket. In the night he woke up, hearing a low murmur of voices.

One of the men was speaking. "Look at it, Jud. Nobody even knows they're alive. And I'd give an arm for that horse."

"What about that Injun?"

"Boy's talk. Iffen there was an Injun, you can bet that b'ar got him."

"Wonder who the boy's pa was?"

"What's it matter? Nobody'll ever hear of it."

"Might recognize the horse."

"We found him astray . . . or swapped him from some Injun. Ain't one chance in a million we'd ever see anybody who'd know the horse. You go to sleep now."

Hardy lay wide awake, staring up at the stars. He was terribly afraid. Once he half sat up, but he saw Cal watching him, and lay down again.

It would be very hard to get away from these two.

7

Daylight came with a chill wind off the mountains, rustling the leaves of the brush, and moaning a little among the pines. The camp lay in an open meadow on the banks of a small stream. There were clumps of willow, a few cottonwoods, and on the slopes of the mountains the golden aspen in thick stands.

Hardy was up, rustling wood for the fire. He was wary now, watching for the slim chance of getting to Big Red, and getting Betty Sue into the saddle. He was frightened, but he told himself he must be brave. He must do what pa would want him to do; but he had no weapon with which to fight these men. He could only wait, and watch for his chance.

At the worst, he might have to run away, even without Betty Sue. That thought was hateful, but for a moment it seemed to him there was little likelihood of their harming her if he was at large and able to testify against them. . . . No, he couldn't bear to think of doing that. Somehow there *had* to be a way to escape. Pa, he said in his thoughts, *pa please come!*

Now, he thought, he would even be glad to see the Indian. Just as the Indian's arrival had given them a chance to escape the grizzly, so his coming now might give them the chance to run away from these men and hide.

He rustled the fire together, and had coffee water on by the time the two men had pulled on their boots.

"This one's quite a hand, Cal," Jud commented. "He's a likely lad around a camp."

Cal did not speak. He looked at the children with a sour expression. It was only when he watched Big Red that his face lit up. "I'm goin' to ride that horse," he said. "I'm goin' to ride him this mornin'."

"Pa don't let anybody ride that horse but him or me," Hardy said.

Cal looked over at him. "You keep your trap shut, boy. Your pa ain't here, an' I'll ride him any time I see fit."

Well, Hardy thought, you take your chances then. Big Red was no horse to fool around with. Hardy remembered when that gangling Peterson boy thought he was a smart aleck. He was going to ride Red whether anybody liked it or not, and the Peterson boy was known as a good rider. . . . Well, he lasted less than a jump, and if he hadn't rolled out between the corral bars he would have been killed.

Maybe that's the way, Hardy thought. Maybe that's the way it will happen.

"Pa will be coming along," he said quietly, "and pa has a way about him."

Jud looked over at him before Cal could speak. "Who is your pa, kid? What's his name?"

"He's at Fort Bridger," Hardy said, "and his name is Scott Collins."

Cal's head turned slowly toward Hardy, his mean eyes staring at him. Hardy thought Jud looked kind of greenish around the gills. "Did you say *Scott Collins?*"

"Yes," said Hardy. "Do you know him?"

"Not exactly . . . we know of him." Jud looked at Hardy. "How's your pa with a shootin' iron, son?"

"He used to win all the turkey shoots back home," Hardy answered. "And folks who served with him during the Indian fighting said he was the best shot they ever did see." Suddenly Hardy remem-

bered a story he had heard Mr. Andy tell around
the fire when he thought Hardy was asleep.

The boy told it now. "One time a bunch of men
came through our part of the country and stole a
cow of pa's, and some stock belonging to some
neighbors. They figured the stock was lost for good,
but pa, he wouldn't say quit. He just set out and
followed those men. It was four months before
he came back, and he had all that stock and the
horses the four men had been riding. He had followed their sign clear down into Missouri.

"Somebody asked pa what would he do if those
men came back hunting their horses, and pa just
grinned and said he never was afraid of ghosts."

Jud looked thoughtful and glanced at Cal, who
shrugged and said, "He's just one man. What he
don't know won't start any wars."

"I don't like it, Cal."

Cal snorted, but Jud was persistent. He looked
over at Hardy. "Yours must've been the last wagon
train west," he said. "This here's late in the season."

"That's what Bill Squires said."

"Squires?"

"He stopped by to do some yarnin', as he said.
He was with us the night before the Indians came,
but he rode off by himself, going west. He promised
Mr. Andy he'd tell pa we were on our way."

"Cal, we better have another think."

"Like hell!"

Jud sliced bacon into the pan, and did not speak
for a moment. Betty Sue huddled close to Hardy
and sipped a little weak coffee.

"If you're figurin' to keep that horse," Jud said
quietly, evidently fearing Cal's irritation, "you'd best
forget about ridin' him now. We'd best saddle up
an' light out."

Cal made no reply to this. He finished his coffee,
got up, and went to his saddle.

"That's my pa's horse!" Hardy protested. "You just
leave him alone!"

"Set down, boy," Jud said harshly. "You get Cal mad an' you'll sure enough find out what meanness is."

Cal threw the blanket on Reds' back and the big stallion side-stepped, but Cal picked up his saddle, threw it on the big horse, and cinched it tight. Then he put the bridle on, and Red stood still for it, chomping and tasting the bit a little.

Cal gathered the reins, put his toe in the stirrup, and threw his leg over. The instant he hit the saddle, Big Red reared straight up, slammed his forefeet down, with his head between his knees, and Cal left the saddle in an arc. He hit the ground in a heap, and Red started for him.

Jud swore and grabbed for his pistol, but Hardy threw himself against Jud's legs, staggering him into losing balance, and he fell.

Jud lunged to his feet, took a swipe at Hardy that knocked him rolling, and reached again for his gun. Cal had rolled over, and he dove for the stream when the stallion came at him. Jud, grabbing for his gun, found only an empty holster.

Looking around quickly, he saw the gun on the ground, and Hardy scrambling to reach it. He kicked the boy, caught up the gun, and wheeled around.

Big Red was gone!

Cal limped from the water, swearing. The side of his face was raw where the skin had been scraped when he landed, and he was soaked to the hide.

"Where'd he go? Where did that—" He stopped, looking around, then turned on Jud. "You damn near let me get killed! Why didn't you shoot him?"

"The kid here bumped me," Jud answered. "Anyway, you're all right."

Hardy was humped over, still gasping for breath. Blood was dripping slowly from his nose, and Betty Sue stared at him in a kind of wide-eyed horror, unable to believe Hardy was hurt, Hardy who had seemed to her strong and invulnerable.

Hardy wanted to cry, but he fought back the tears. What was it pa said? "You've got to think, son. *Think!*" As he hugged his arms to his aching body his eyes searched the brush around. He was bent over so they could not see his face, and they were talking now, seeming almost to forget him.

Big Red would not go far, Hardy told himself. He was out there, somewhere. If they could only—

"Give me your horse," Cal was saying. "I'll go find that red devil, an' when I do I'll throw and hog-tie him. Before he gets up he'll know who's boss!"

"Go ahead," Jud replied, with a meaning glance. "I'll take care of things here."

Cal saddled up and rode out, but Jud sat down and drank coffee. Occasionally he looked over at Betty Sue. Hardy crawled back near her and sat up, holding himself tight.

"Busted a rib, mebbe," Jud commented maliciously. "Serves you right."

He picked up the coffeepot, sloshed the coffee around, and drank from the side of the pot, then he put the pot down and wiped the back of his hand across his mouth. He picked up the bacon and wrapped it up, then ran his hunting knife into the ground a couple of times to clean it off.

Hardy bumped against Betty Sue. "Run!" he whispered. "Run hard!"

Betty Sue got to her feet. She was frightened, and she was not too good a runner, for she was scarcely more than a baby. Hardy was worried about her getting away, but he knew he couldn't carry her and run too.

Jud turned around, knife in hand, a cold, ugly look in his eyes.

"*Now!*" Hardy yelled shrilly, and Betty Sue started to run for the bushes.

Jud swore and started to turn to go after her, and Hardy threw himself against his legs. Again the man fell, but Hardy was up first, and was running too. He crashed into the bushes an instant before Betty Sue, and turned and dragged her into some kind of game tunnel. Jud was coming after them, swearing and shouting.

Hardy crawled through the tunnel, which was scarcely large enough for him, and reached the bank of the stream. He picked up Betty Sue and ran stumbling along the river bank where it was partly clear.

Jud, unable to follow through the tunnel, was coming around the bushes, coming fast. But Hardy had played too many games in the woods with the boys not to know every ruse.

"Betty Sue!" he yelled. "This way!" Then he turned and started back the way they had come, remembering a place in the stream where he had seen a sandy bottom and some stepping stones.

They got across the stream and into the trees without being seen and gasping for breath, he put Betty Sue down. Pain was stabbing at his side, but he didn't think anything was broken—it was just a bad bruise. He had been bruised like that before, the time he had tried to ride old Brindle's calf, and the calf threw him. Only this hurt more.

They walked away from the stream, and dodged from bush to bush on the slope until they came to a grove of aspen. They crawled in among the trees, needing little space in which to hide.

After a bit, they peered out. Jud was walking along the river bank, studying it for tracks. Soon he found them and crossed the stream, hunting along the near bank for some sign of the children.

It was very still. Hardy could hear Betty Sue's breathing as she lay beside him in their hiding place. The air was clear, and he could hear small twigs cracking under Jud's feet as he searched. Hardy lay there, his heart pounding, and tried to think what to do. Was it better to lie still and hope that Jud could not find them, or to try and get further up the hill and risk being seen? A moving object attracts the eye; pa had taught him that.

The hill behind them was steep, and Hardy had an idea he could outrun Jud going uphill, but he knew that Betty Sue could not. And she was too heavy for him to carry more than a few feet.

Jud had rushed at first; now he was settling down to work out their trail. But there was a chance that he was not as good a tracker as pa or Bill Squires. . . .

And where was Big Red?

Hardy could smell the dark earth beneath them, and the leaves. Above them the aspen trembled unceasingly. There was a legend about that . . . what was it?

Now it seemed that Jud had lost the trail, and had gone back to try to work it out.

"Watch him," Hardy whispered, then eased back in the aspens and found a place where he could look up the slope. He needed to locate a place they could get to without being seen. After a moment, he found it.

As was often the case in such places, the slope of the mountain was dotted with small clusters of aspen, growing so compactly that in many places only a child or small animal could crawl in among them with any ease.

Not over fifty yards up and further along the slope was another aspen grove, and there were clumps of brush here and there, all with the bright colors of autumn. And rocks were scattered about. With luck, they could make it unseen.

He started to hiss to Betty Sue, but then remembered how easily sound carried. He slipped back, touched her and they started up.

It was only about twenty feet to the nearest rock and they made it easily, concealed from below by the aspens they had just left. Squirming along the ground, they got to a clump of brush, and then they waited until Jud's back was turned and sprinted for the next clump. They reached it just as he swung his head around, perhaps drawn by some faint sound.

Hardy studied the valley below with care, but there was still no sign of Big Red.

On the slightly hollowed surface of a rock they found some water from the recent rains, and scooped it up with their hands to get a drink. Watching from the rock, they could see Jud was almost up to their first hiding place, so they moved on, going higher and higher.

They were cold, and it was clouding up again. But most of all, Hardy was worried about Big Red. He was afraid of what Cal might do if he managed to rope and tie the horse; but he also knew that without the horse he and Betty Sue were not going very far.

He had never felt so tired, and more than anything he wanted to curl up in some warm place and just sleep. But first they had to get safely away from Cal and Jud, and they had to find Red. Pa loved that horse as much as Hardy did, and Red was Hardy's responsibility.

Jud wasn't much of a tracker. Apparently he had given up in disgust, and was just looking around at random. Hardy and Betty Sue did not weigh much, and their feet were small, so that they made little impression on the ground or the grass. An Indian would have had no trouble following them, but Jud was no Indian, and he was lazy. He knew the children could not have gone far, so if he just went from one possible hiding place to another along the slope, he felt that he could find them.

Hardy could see just what Jud was beginning to do: and the worst of it was, it would work. And if they started out to run, Jud could catch them—at least, he could catch Betty Sue.

Keeping a grove of aspens between them and Jud, they climbed higher. Up there, in the shadow of a rock, Hardy saw a little snow. He had seen it up on the mountains, but here, so close to them, it was different, and it frightened him. They were much higher up now than they had been before, and tonight it would be cold, and they would have no blanket.

That was when the idea came to him. Instead of just running away from them, why not give Jud and Cal something to worry about? Suppose, while Cal was following the stallion and Jud was hunting for them, they slipped back and robbed Jud's camp?

Stealing was wrong; but this was war, and if Jud caught them now they would be killed, Hardy knew that. He had known that was what the men intended to do from that conversation he had overheard that first night.

If he could worry them enough, he could make them afraid to leave their camp to look for either Big Red or for Betty Sue and himself.

As if in answer to his thinking, he saw a deep groove cut by a runlet of snow water coming off the mountain. It was not deep enough to hide the movements of a man, but it was perfect for them. Hardy took Betty Sue by the hand and they crept toward it.

8

It was Scott Collins who found the first sign of the grizzly. He indicated it to the others without comment. They all knew what it might mean. It was a little over an hour later that they came upon the scene of the titanic battle.

The ground was torn by the marks of the stallion's hoofs and the paw marks of the grizzly. Here and there they also found the footprints of the children, most of them Hardy's. The carcass of the bear, torn somewhat by scavenging coyotes, lay in the deepest brush.

"Those youngsters are shot with luck," Darrow said grimly. "Wonder that bear didn't do 'em in."

"Look here." Collins tugged the boy's arrow from the bear's throat. "That's no Indian arrow. Hardy got in one shot, anyway."

Slowly, methodically, as was their way, they put the story together. They could see the tracks, they could see the wounds in the bear's body, and they could imagine what had happened. These were men of the mountains and the prairie, who read trail sign as an educated man reads print.

The torn earth, the swirling, twisting hoof marks of the stallion were plain enough; so were the gashes in the bear's hide. But the gashes were only superficial wounds, nothing that could have seriously hampered the bear. There was no obvious evidence of the kick in the ribs that the bear had received, but even that proved little. The grizzly

73

bear, the largest of flesh-eating creatures, is, when cornered, the fiercest.

The one thing they looked at, and at first avoided thinking about, was the deep slash in the bear's breast. Somebody with a knife had cut open the dead bear and ripped out its heart.

Finally Bill Squires pointed to it. "That's an Injun trick," he said. "He eats the bear's heart to get his strength and fierceness. On'y there's somethin' else here . . . somethin' must've made that Injun figure this bear was strong medicine."

"This isn't finding Hardy," Scott Collins said after a moment. "We'd best be getting on."

"They're ridin' again," Darrow said from across the clearing. "The stallion took out of here like he was rode."

The evidence of the trail proved him correct. The steady, even gait of the stallion showed that he was ridden by someone.

They followed the trail. It was vague here and there, almost gone in some places, and unraveling it was a problem. But there were three men to scatter out to pick up leads, and they kept on, traveling slower than Hardy had, but pushing on all the time.

Scott was far off to one side when Squires hailed him. "Hey, look at this!" he called.

Darrow and Scott rode over and studied the fresh sign—two mounted horses and a pack outfit.

Squires took out his tobacco and bit off a chew, then squinted his eyes at Scott. "You see what I see?"

"I see." Collins studies the tracks closely. "Those tracks were made by that piebald gelding of Ben Starr's."

"Uh-huh . . . and what d'you know about that piebald?"

"Hell," Darrow said, remembering, "he was stolen."

"I ought to know those tracks," Squires said. "It was me swapped him that horse."

Those two riders were making no effort to conceal their trail, and they evidently did not fear pursuit. It was late in the season for them to be traveling in the area, and pursuit was unlikely here, even if they were suspected.

"If we ride behind 'em long enough," Squires said, "we'll sure enough know who they be. It ain't as if this country was full of folks, an' I been here long enough to know most of 'em. Why, I come into this country so early Jim Bridger was considered a tenderfoot. Weren't many ahead of me . . . 'cept John Coulter an' them."

The valley in which they now rode was wide, cut by many small streams and crossed by at least one river; and another river flowed down from the north. There were towering mountains off to the east, and high mountains closer by, to the west. Even now, in late September, it was a green and lovely land, with trout leaping in the rivers and wild game everywhere.

The three men had found the markers left by Hardy, so they knew he had taken this way. "He's tryin' to git away," Darrow said. "I reckon he knew that Injun was behind him."

"He's got more trouble," Scott Collins commented. He had been worrying about this for some time. "If those men who are trailing him would steal the piebald, they'd steal my stallion too—if they don't get killed trying. That stallion doesn't take to strangers. He never did."

Twice they lost the trail, and twice they found it again. The track of the stallion was easy enough to follow when Hardy made no effort to conceal it.

It was dusk when they found the ashes of a campfire.

"No use trying to see anything tonight," said Squires. "Walk back the way we came so's we won't mess up the ground."

About fifty yards away, they made camp, and Scott could not restrain himself—he was sure they were close, so very sure. He went out a ways from the camp and called . . . a dozen times he called into the night, but there was no answer.

"He's goin' to take it hard," Darrow commented to Bill Squires, "if we don't find that boy."

"We *got* to find him," Squires said. "That there's a good man . . . and, come to think of it, that's quite a youngster, too."

"Scott sure enough put the run on those claim-jumpers back at Hangtown. Sent the lot of 'em packin'." Darrow grinned. "All but Dub Holloway."

"Holloway convinced 'em," Squires said. "Holloway was goin' to take his measure. And he sure did . . . trouble was he didn't live to see it."

Scott Collins finally came back to camp. "The way I see it," he said, "those horse stealers came upon the stallion's tracks. If they followed very far they'd soon know there was only a couple of young ones riding him. What happened then depends on what kind of men they are."

"Ain't many would do harm to a youngster," Darrow said. "There wouldn't be a place they'd dare show their face."

"If it was found out," Squires responded. "Look at it. The kids are out here alone. They'd have no idea we were huntin' 'em. There's on'y that Injun to know."

It was a quiet camp. Squires smoked a pipe, and after that he turned in. Frank Darrow tried to make talk of the trail and the country around, but finally he gave up. Only Scott Collins remained awake and stayed up. He could not have slept anyway, and there was always the chance he might hear something.

After a little while he moved out from camp and sat down in the darkness to listen.

This was Indian country, although not very many Indians were wandering now. At any time snow could close the country in, and any Indian in his right mind preferred the warmth of his lodge and a squaw to feed him and keep his fire going. The Utes, the Bannocks, the Cheyennes and the Black-feet all rode through here. The Shoshone too, for that matter; and occasionally, in good weather, the Crows.

The air was clear, and the night was cold. On such nights, and in such air, sound carried a long distance, so Scott sat out there alone and listened. What he feared was that if the children were alive they might be carried off by some wandering party of Indians. The Utes might take them far down in-to Colorado or Utah; the Cheyennes might go back north to the mountains.

The stars were very bright. Once he heard a beaver tail slap the still waters of his pond, and a wolf howled. It was not a coyote . . . that was a wolf, a big one, a timber wolf.

There was that to worry about, too. Many a wild animal that would not dare attack a man might attack a child.

At daybreak he was back at camp; Darrow was putting together some breakfast. Around the camp-fire they worked out the events that had taken place.

"Horse throwed him an' got away," Squires said. After a while he added, "Those youngsters got away, too. Seems like."

Scott looked at Squires. "You read it the way I do?" he asked.

"Looks like your boy got some rough treatment, near's a body can see. Thing is, they all got away. Now, if that horse was a mustang he'd trace that boy. I see a mustang foller a trail like a blood-hound."

"Red does all right. I've seen him follow the boy when he went hunting. Did you ever see a horse like to go hunting?"

"Uh-huh. Had a pony one time who'd come up

behind me an' hang his head right over my shoulder when I was about to shoot."

"How long ago?" Scott queried, indicating the sign. "Two days?"

"Looks like. No longer'n three. We gained on 'em some, I figure."

On the slope above the camp they lost all trace of the two children. Leaving one of the clumps of aspen, they had come out on a wide shelf of native rock swept free of soil by a long-ago landslide. The two children had gone across that rock like ghosts, and left no trail behind.

"What do we do now?" Darrow asked.

"Try to find the stallion. He's pretty sure to be with the children."

"I'd like to come up to those men," Collins said grimly.

"I know one of 'em," Darrow admitted suddenly. "I can't place 'im, but I know 'im."

"What's that mean?"

"I don't know myself, except that I was in a camp with one of those men sometime or other. I recognized the way things were around camp . . . you know, a man gets into habits."

"You can't recall his name? It might help."

"I'll think of it. It'll come to me."

They rode on. Now the trail was more difficult to follow, for the two riders had spread out, trying to find the stallion's hoofprints.

"It's familiar country," Bill Squires commented. "We made rendezvous one time just south of Horse Creek near the Green. Near as I can recall it was July, 1837. That's eleven years ago now, but it don't seem so long a time."

He squinted his eyes at the mountains. "We better find those youngsters quick. She's comin' on to cold."

"We'll find them. I can feel it now," Collins said.

It was a lovely land in the crisp autumn air, the sunlight dancing on the creek waters, and the golden aspen twinkling in its rustling movement. Here and there the red of other leaves was like a splash of blood across the flank of the mountain.

Now the land grew rougher. Deep gorges opening out from the mountain sides were like raw wounds in the earth. Often they saw deer, and once a small herd of elk. There were wolf tracks and cougar tracks, and the marks of beaver teeth.

"We nearly trapped 'em out in the spring of '37 and the fall of '36," Squires said. "We had to keep an eye out for Blackfeet too. They were cruising this country, and there was no friendship amongst us in those days.

"I was with Joe Meek, Osborne Russell, and them when we had the big fight. They nearly licked us, too. And nearly everybody in those times had 'im a brush with grizzlies. Russell and me come up a stream up Yellowstone way . . . I forget the year . . . and saw eight or nine grizzlies standin' up on their hind legs jest a-eatin' berries for all they was worth. They paid us no mind, just went on eatin'.'"

Scott Collins drew up. He could see the tracks of the children clearly enough, and superimposed on them the tracks of the stallion.

"Red's trailing them!" he called to Squires, who had ridden off a few feet to check the earth around a flat stone.

"They rested a while here," Squires said. "I figured when I saw that rock, 'Now, if I was a boy, an' tired, where would I set?' An' sure enough, there they'd been."

Scott leaned over and looked at the tracks when he drew alongside. He was a man very easy in his movements, but quick to move when the occasion demanded. He studied the ground while Squires offered a running commentary.

"The little one, she's tried. Draggin' her feet more'n we've been seein' her do. But look there now. The boy's got himself some sort of pack. See where he put it down?"

Squires chuckled. "You know what I'm thinkin'? That boy snuck back into their camp whilst they hunted 'im, an' he made off with some of their grub. Leastways, that's what I hope he done."

They followed along. Scott Collins took the lead now. He fought back the worry that rode him relentlessly, trying to keep an objective view so he would not be persuaded one way or the other. A man could read both too much and too little into a trail, and until now the children had been both fortunate in finding a little something to eat, and unfortunate in those they met, animal or man.

He could hope, yet he dared not let himself hope too much. "I'll find them," he told himself. "I've got to find them." He remembered to be proud of his son. The boy had learned his lessons well, and was recalling now things he needed to know.

In midafternoon they lost the trail at a small stream. It was gone completely where a herd of elk had wandered across it and, perhaps frightened by something, had milled about a good deal. Then they had wandered on, leaving no sign behind that helped.

The men searched across the grass of the meadow, cropped over and trodden by deer and elk, and apparently even by a few buffalo, rare in that region. They found nothing they could identify as a track of horse or man. Once, near a bush, they thought they found what might have been a moccasin print, one vague side of a footprint which they could not decide upon as human. Children, horse, and their pursuers had vanished as if caught up by the wind.

Scattered out, the three men rode on. They had seen trails peter out before, and had found them again, so they were not too discouraged. There was still good grass, and the streams running off the mountain were clear and bright, but they found no place where a horse had fed, and no horse tracks along the streams where they searched.

"I got to be pullin' out soon." Frank Darrow spoke reluctantly. A gruff, hard-bitten man, he held few illusions and only one loyalty . . . that was to his friends. "I got to think of my stock, with winter comin' on." He glanced at Scott. "Ain't like I want to leave you in the lurch."

"I know it, Frank. You go along when you're ready."

Their camp was somber that night, and there was no talk around the fire. All three were now feeling depressed by losing the trail and not finding it again as they had expected.

"They turned off," Darrow said. "I figure they turned off somewheres, the whole kit an' kaboodle of 'em."

They discussed the possibilities, weighing each one. They had to put themselves in the minds of the children, had to imagine what they would do.

"I doubt they'd tackle the mountain," Squires said. "It looks almighty hard."

"Hardy might," Scott said after a moment. "He always liked to climb, and he might try to go where they'd not expect him to go. And he'd try his best to point toward Bridger."

None of them wanted to turn back now, but all of them felt they had come too far, and so at last they turned away from the camp. With every step Scott worried for fear they were abandoning his son and the child of his friend. He knew, as they all did, that the time for searching with any hope was almost at an end. It was time for the winter storms to sweep through the valley, to cloak the mountains with snow; and then no lightly clad child could be expected to live.

There was no question of hurrying, for to hurry now meant losing the trail completely, a trail more difficult to find with every passing hour.

Scott Collins knew this land, and loved it, but he knew every danger it offered. He knew, too, the ways to avoid trouble and the ways to survive. You could not war against the wilderness; to live in it one must become a part of it, make oneself one with the trees and the wind, the streams and the plants, the cold and the heat, yielding a little always, but never too much.

Now, for the first time, he really appreciated the hard struggle he and Hardy had had to live at all. Nothing had been easy on the farm where Hardy had begun growing up. One survived only through work and because of work. At night when cold winter winds howled about their cabin, it had been warm and snug inside, but only because of the care with which he had built it. He had done nothing slip-shod, everything had been done with as meticulous care as possible.

He had shaped each beam, notched each log, placed each stone of the fireplace with his own hands, and he had fitted them tightly, knowing the icy fingers of the cold would find every crack, every crevice.

He had always been a careful workman, and he had tried to give Hardy the one thing that is needed above all, a sense of responsibility. He had sometimes wished that Hardy need not come to the forest with him when it was cold, or when it was too hot. He had wished the boy might have had it a bit easier, but now he was glad he had not.

Hardy had learned in a hard school, where the tests are given by savage Indians, by bitter cold, by hunger. These were tests where the result was not just a bad mark if one failed. The result was a starved or frozen body somewhere, forgotten in the wilderness.

The men rode into a basin where a large lake lay at the bottom of a depression north of the Sweetwater. Scott put a fire together, while Squires

set about rustling some grub. Scott had killed a
deer that morning, so they did not lack for meat.

Frank Darrow rode out from camp. Two hours
later, when the others had eaten, he rode in and
swung down, stripping the gear from his horse.

"Picked up some sign," he said over a cup of
coffee. "That red stallion had himself a drink t'other
side of the lake."

"Any other sign?" Scott was almost afraid to ask.
"Are the youngsters with him?"

Frank Darrow took a big bite of frying pan
bread, and chewed methodically, while Bill
Squires's eyes started to twinkle.

"Uh-huh," Darrow said, no longer able to repress
a grin. "They're with 'im. Somehow or t'other
they found each other. It was yestiddy mornin',
near as a body could figure."

He gulped hot coffee. "We got to hurry," he said.
"Those others weren't far behind 'em." And after a
minute he added, "The stallion's got a saddle on
him now, so the kid can get up on him when he's
of a mind to. So one o' them others is ridin' bareback . . . I seen the place where he mounted up
again."

"Maybe tomorrow then," Squires said. "I'm lookin' forward to meetin' up with those gents."

9

Nobody was in camp when Hardy Collins crawled up through the brush and studied the layout. He waited long enough to be sure it was not a trap; to wait longer might give them time to return. He did not ask himself if he was doing a wrong thing, for the men had talked of stealing Big Red and killing Betty Sue and himself. Moreover, the men had plenty of grub, and he did not intend that Betty Sue should go hungry when bad men had more than enough.

He planned every move before he started from the brush, and once he emerged in the open he worked swiftly. A slab of bacon into a burlap sack, a pound of coffee, a pound or so of sugar, above five pounds of pilot bread, and maybe four pounds, as near as he could guess, of dried fruit. It made a heavy load, but when he got it to the brush he left it hidden there and returned to camp.

Hastily, he rummaged through everything, but he could find nothing to shoot with. There was ammunition enough, but . . . Then he found it—a U.S. Army derringer, .41 caliber. He checked quickly to see if it was loaded, then he stuffed it down in his pocket.

There was a movement in the brush, and he turned and fled, ducking into the opening in the brush almost without slowing down. Once inside, he took hold of the sack and dragged it after him. On the other side of the heavy growth he shouldered the sack and, keeping to low ground, he worked his way back to where Betty Sue waited. Together they trudged off.

If Big Red was to find them—and he could find them much more easily than they could find him —they must leave a trail he could follow. To do that, they must, he decided, walk right straight across the valley. In that way the horse would come upon their trail. For Red had run away to the north—at least, he was heading north when last they saw him—so if he started back he must cross their trail.

Having taken a sighting on a peak, Hardy started off, holding to as straight a course as possible. Betty Sue walked beside him.

"Get something to eat?" Betty Sue asked, after a while.

"Don't you worry. We'll eat tonight," Hardy said, "and Big Red will find us. You can figure on it. Why, I can't number the times he's traipsed into the woods after me, and sometimes I'd hide out from him, but he'd find me, ever' time."

They went down into the bed of a stream, but this time they did not follow through the water, although it was shallow enough for wading. Instead, they walked through the grass along the banks, and Hardy frequently wetted his feet in the water, hoping to make the scent more lasting.

When they had gone no more than two miles, Hardy saw Betty Sue lagging. He was afraid to stop so soon, but he knew she could not go any farther. In a deep, wooded hollow near the stream he made a small fire and broiled some bacon over the coals. They ate this, and each of them ate a small piece of the pilot bread. Then they carefully put out the fire, and Hardy led Betty Sue to a thick grove of aspen on the slope above them. Between the aspen and a cluster of rocks they made a bed and lay down.

The wind blew cold on the mountain, and the aspen leaves rustled. Betty Sue was soon asleep, but Hardy lay awake a long time, listening for Big Red.

He had always taken responsibilities seriously, but now in the lonely night he was frightened, fearful of the strange sounds, of mysterious rustlings, of the movements of prowling creatures. In the night he thought of pa, and he remembered Mr. Andy and his slow, purposeful ways. Mr. Andy never seemed to hurry, but he was always busy, always getting something done, and he had many skills. As pa said, Mr. Andy was the kind of man the frontier needed.

Pa himself was a driver. He moved more quickly, but just as surely. He was a man who knew what he wanted, and never stopped working to get it. If he failed along one line, he was always ready to proceed on another.

Hardy realized that he had learned some good things from pa; one was to do one thing at a time; not to cross bridges until he came to them, but at the same time to try to imagine how he could cross them when the time came. Though he was scared now, he was scared less for himself than for Betty Sue, for it was always in his mind how helpless she would be if anything happened to him.

He knew she trusted in him, and believed in him completely. And that made him remember something else pa had told him: that a body never knew how strong he could be until somebody expected it of him.

He tried to figure how far they must be from Fort Bridger now. As well as he could figure, they were somewhere in the foothills of the Wind River Mountains, and Bridger was way beyond there. He knew he had to keep out of the mountains, because everybody talked about how awful it was to get snowed in . . . and snow could come almighty sudden. Tomorrow, when he made the slope of the mountains, he would have to turn and follow along them.

Betty Sue didn't talk much. She was so tired when they came to bed down at night that she fell asleep right off, and during the daytime they had to ride quiet most of the time . . . or walk quiet. He was glad they had not had much talk, for she was always so filled with questions, and he was in no position to answer her questions now. He could not even answer his own.

But she must not know how frightened he was, or how little he actually could do. She must keep her complete trust in him, for without it she had nothing.

Somewhere in these thoughts he fell asleep, and for four hours he slept well. When he woke up suddenly it was still dark. Two things had brought him out of his sound sleep. One was the light, feathery, cool touch of a snowflake on his cheek; the other was a sound, the faintest of sounds.

He lay perfectly still. One hand felt for the pistol tucked in his pocket.

Another snowflake touched his cheek, and then another, and another.

He lay there listening. Again he heard a faint stir on the slope below them; something was moving down there, ever so carefully. Very quietly he sat up and tugged on his boots. Betty Sue slept on, shivering a little under his old coat.

The night was velvety soft, but there were no stars. Nearby the aspens whispered to the gentle wind. Hardy waited, his heart pounding, listening for the surreptitious movements on the slope below them. At last, shivering with cold, he lay down again and cuddled close to Betty Sue.

But he did not stay there long, for he thought of the snow falling, and of the tracks they would leave. They could not be very far from where Cal and Jud had camped. The thought gave him an idea, and he sat up again, listening.

This time he heard no sound and after listening a little longer he crept around to the side of the clump of aspen behind which they had found shelter. Out across the valley he saw a faint red glow. Without doubt it was a campfire; it might be a mile off, or even more. He was well above the valley, and he could see such a light from some distance away.

Suddenly his scalp prickled. There was a slight movement close behind him. He stood for an instant, frozen in fear, and then he knew what he had to do. He must jump straight ahead and try to scramble through the brush.

At that instant something prickly and wet touched him on the neck. He seemed to jump inside his skin, barely stifling an outcry, and at the same moment there came realization.

It was Big Red. He had found them.

Hardy put an arm around Big Red's lowered neck and hugged him close, and then he started to cry, struggling all the while to fight back the tears. It was not the manly thing to do, but he couldn't help it.

He knew at once what they must do. They must leave now, before snow covered the ground, they must leave before there were any tracks to find. If they did this, they might leave Cal and Jud behind them for good, and that big Indian too, if he was still back there.

Hardy led the horse back to Betty Sue and shook her awake. Hoisting her to the saddle—for Red still wore Cal's saddle—Hardy put the sack of food up and then climbed up himself. There were rocks enough here for him to stand on, but with the saddle a rock was no longer necessary.

It was completely dark, but he had only to follow along the slope, keeping the mountain on his right side, and when they reached the southern end of the Wind River chain, to go south and around the tip and then head west.

Big Red needed no guiding. Seemingly happy to find them again, he started off along the mountain at a fast, space-eating walk. Hardy hunched his thin shoulders against the cold and hung the reins on the pommel. With an arm on either side of Betty Sue, he clung to the saddle-forks.

After a while he even dozed a little, and the big horse walked steadily on into the night.

10

By the time day broke, the snow was falling steadily, and Hardy was blue with cold. He turned Big Red toward a row of trees that seemed to indicate nearby water, and when they came to a stream he followed along it, seeking shelter of any kind at all.

It was sheer luck that he glimpsed the half-open door of the dugout.

The door was hidden behind a huge, leaning cottonwood; when the tree leafed out, it would be invisible. It was a crudely made door of split cottonwood, and was hung on leather hinges.

All about the place, and along the bank of the small stream, the only tracks were those of animals and birds. Warily, Hardy rode up and, hanging to the stirrup strap, slid to the ground.

Pulling the door open a little wider, he peered in. It was a deserted but snug little place. In one wall was a fireplace, utilizing a natural hole, enlarged with a pick or an axe, for a chimney. A double bunk had been built along the right-hand wall, and nearby was a block of wood that had evidently done its turn as a chair or table. The top of it was polished, apparently from much sitting.

Packrats had been around—at least Hardy supposed that was what they were—and the place was dusty and seemed long-abandoned.

He helped Betty Sue down, and rubbed her cold little hands between his own, making them both warmer. Then he took his knife and went out to look around.

Farther along the bank he found an overhang where the unknown occupant—perhaps a miner or trapper—had stabled his horse. The place was sheltered from wind and snow, and it was also well concealed by willows and cottonwoods. He picketed the stallion there, the rope permitting the horse to move from the stream to the overhang.

Then Hardy went back to the dugout and, gathering sticks from the packrats' nest, he kindled a fire. There was wood enough outside, some of it from fallen trees, some of it driftwood brought downstream and cast up against rocks or brush on the bank.

When Hardy had a good fire going, he began to poke about. He found a frying pan, an old iron kettle, an old pick, with the handle almost gnawed away by porcupines or some other wild creatures for the salty taste left by sweaty hands.

Somebody had spent a good deal of time working on the place. "Looks to me," he said to Betty Sue, "as if somebody holed up here quite a spell. He surely knew how to do for himself," he added. "This here is a kind of natural cave which he made bigger by knocking off chunks of rock here and there. Even that chimney was a natural hole in the rocks."

He took the kettle and the frying pan to the stream and washed both of them with wood ashes, which took the place of soap, and scoured them with sand. After he rinsed them they looked pretty good, and would do for heating water and frying bacon.

He went back to the dugout, where the fire was making it warm, and held his cold hands out to the blaze. As they warmed up they prickled as if little needles were sticking in them. When they were really warm again he got out the bacon and sliced several slices into the pan, then put some water on in the kettle to boil. Several times he made quick dashes out into the cold to get armfuls of wood to put beside the fireplace so they would have a good supply. He found that he could shut the door, and there was a bar for it, but he felt almost guilty about being so warm inside when he had to leave Big Red outside.

The dugout was shaped like a triangle with one point lopped off, and the door was where the point would have been. The room was no more than eight feet deep, but the firelight scarcely reached the gloom of the opposite wall. The fireplace side of the wall was very rough, and some of the projections of rock had been used as small shelves.

When Hardy had fried the bacon the water was boiling, and he dropped the coffee into it. After they had eaten the bacon and a piece of pilot bread apiece, he dropped a little cold water into the kettle to settle the grounds, and they took turns drinking from the kettle, Hardy holding the kettle with a piece of old sacking so as not to burn his hands.

Rummaging about in the back of the dugout, he found that at the head of the bunk there was a tight wooden door in the wall. He opened it and, holding a brand from the fire, studied the small interior. On the floor lay a tightly wrapped pack of furs, much gnawed, and on sticks thrust into the wall there hung a pair of old jeans, worn and patched, a couple of folded blankets, very dusty and moth eaten, and a huge old buffalo coat. This, although difficult of access by animals, for it touched the wall nowhere, was somewhat chewed around the collar.

Taking the coat outside—and it was so heavy that moving it was a struggle—he threw it over a bush after knocking off the snow, and proceeded to beat dust from it with a stick. Extra large as it was, it would do to sleep under, and it would cover them both while riding.

The blankets were of little use, or so he thought at first. But after beating dust from them in the gathering twilight, he suddenly had an idea. With his knife, he cut pieces from one of them that would make a sort of cape for Betty Sue and one for himself.

The other blanket, which was in somewhat better shape, he took outside, and by working a strip of rawhide he found in the dugout through the many holes, he had a blanket that would at least partly cover Big Red.

Now, for the first time in days they were really warm. A cold wind came in under the door from time to time, but otherwise it was pleasant and almost cheerful.

"Hardy, when will we get to For' Brid'er?" Betty Sue asked.

"Soon."

"Will mama be there?"

"She might be. I hope so."

She was silent a moment. "I like this place. It's warm."

"I like it, too." He remembered the falling snow. "Maybe we'll stay here until the storm is over," he added.

He had not considered it until that moment, but he knew right away that it was the thing to do. They had food enough for two or three days of resting and waiting for the snow to stop, and a little less for the rest of the trip.

Outside the snow continued to fall steadily. The world had turned white, with the snow covering the trees, bending down the heavily laden branches, and wiping out any trail they had left. When they had finished eating, Hardy put on his blanket-cape and went out to carry in wood for the fires. He found driftwood, and many dry branches broken from deadfalls. He took some of it inside, and stacked the rest near the door.

Though he was terribly tired and his feet were

dragging, he forced himself to keep going. After all, he was only seven, and there was so much for him to do, but he remembered that pa had often told him that the way to succeed in life was just to keep trying . . . and to keep faith. He knew what that meant, even though he could not have put it in words.

From time to time he stopped in the overhang shelter to talk to Big Red, and to pat him. The snow made it light outside and he worked long after night had come, until at last he was too tired to do any more. Then he dragged himself back to the dugout and closed and barred the door behind him.

The fire kept the place warm. Though a little cold air came in under the door, he knew they would need that much ventilation, and when they sat on the bunk, their feet dangling, they were warm and snug, and were not hungry.

"You wait," Hardy said to Betty Sue, "pa will come. If he isn't hunting us now, he's waiting for us at Bridger. I know my pa, and if we don't come soon, I know he'll be looking for us."

But even as he spoke he knew that, even if the wagon train had been moving steadily westward, it probably could not have been at Bridger yet, though it might have been getting close. He had no reason to believe pa knew anything had happened to it, or to Hardy and Betty Sue. But he would not be long in finding out.

Pa was like that. He never took anything for granted, and he always set out to learn all he could. You could bet that by the time he had reached Bridger he had heard all anybody knew about conditions along the Overland Trail; he might even imagine what could happen to the children.

"A man lives by what he knows," he used to tell Hardy. "Try to get all the facts, and study them, and you can usually make out. When I was a boy, apprenticed to a millwright, he could make me

check every measurement, study every piece of
lumber we used. If he taught me anything, it was
to learn all I could about whatever I was doing."

Back there in Wisconsin, when other folks
shunned the Indians pa was always out there talking to them. Those Indians, he used to tell Hardy,
had lived in that country a long time before the
white man came, and they knew a lot worth learning. Pa went to the woods with them and, when
Hardy was old enough, he took him along.

It was a time of warring for the Indians. A lot of
folks had the idea that the Indians lived together
in peace until the white man came, but times of
peace were rare among them. The Sioux and the
Chippewas were always fighting and raiding back
and forth. Many a time Hardy himself had seen
painted Indians slipping through the woods
headed north or south on the warpath.

"One time," he told Betty Sue, "pa and me had
been to Fort Snelling. Pa, he had business there
with Major Greenleaf Dearborn—some kind of
building work. I can just recall it, but I do remember seeing the Dragoons on parade, the flags and
everything. It's about the earliest thing I do remember.

"Only on the way back, pa and me ran into a
war party of Winnebagos. There must have been
twenty or thirty of them, and we hid under a river
bank, with them right close above us. We could
hear them talking. They had seen our tracks and,
come daylight, they would try to round us up for
our scalps and for pa's rifle gun."

"What did you do?" Betty Sue asked.

"I only remember what pa told me, and not
much else. I recall hiding under that bank, though,
and pa with his hand over my mouth, and then I
recall how pa put me in one of their canoes and
he took his hand-axe and cut holes in the bottom
of all the other canoes. He got off in the one
canoe, and they shot at us. I remember their guns

going off, and pa putting down his paddle to
shoot."

Hardy stared into the fire, thinking back to how
he had gone with pa when pa worked in the lumber woods on Rum River, and how pa had helped
change over a mill from a flutter mill to an over-
shot mill.

The two of them had spent a lot of time walking
through the woods from place to place. The only
way pa could make any cash money was to work
at his trade, and he was good at it.

The officers at Fort Snelling and Fort Atkinson
wanted to fix up their quarters, and they were
allowed to do it if they stood the expense themselves, and pa had done much of the work. The
trouble was, it meant neglecting the farm, and
pa didn't like to do that.

Hardy had liked it when they traveled. The
woods were dark and deep, and there was a mix-
ture of evergreen trees and those that dropped
their leaves in the fall of the year. There was a
great variety—sugar maple and elm, oak, butter-
nut, white and black ash, wild plum, birch, hack-
berry, and cedar; Hardy knew them all. Farther
north there were the pines and spruce. There were
nuts and berries too—the beaked hazelnut like the
ones he'd found back yonder, and blueberries,
wild currants, and crab apples.

Many a time they lived off the country, gathering
herbs, picking nuts or berries, and shooting game.
A knowing man could live well in the forest, and
it had taken pa no time at all to learn what the
Indians knew. He took to the wild country like a
man born to it, and to tracking as if he'd lived with
it all his life. A good deal of it rubbed off on Hardy.
He watched and he listened and he helped. For a
boy full of questions, it was a grand way to live.

Pa read to him, too, but mostly Hardy learned
from the book of the forest and the book of men.
The latter learning came to him from listening to

pa talk with other men about farming and hunting, or about their work, and from hearing pa's comments on places and people.

They hadn't much to read, although there was some exchanging of books. Pa had come west with a Bible, *Pilgrim's Progress, Scottish Chiefs,* and *Ivanhoe.* When Mr. Andy finally joined up with them, he had *Thaddeus of Warsaw,* by Porter, and *Castle Rackrent,* by Maria Edgeworth. At night, by the fire, pa read to him from the books and started teaching him his letters.

One time when they had gone to Fort Snelling to work on some building there, Major Dearborn had loaned pa a copy of *Marmion* and a new book, published only a few years before, Carlyle's *History of the French Revolution.* The two books lasted the winter through, and *Marmion* they read three times, from beginning to end.

Often they would be on the road, usually walking for four or five days at a stretch, and Hardy and his pa being together they talked man talk.

"About all a man can leave his boy," pa had said, "is the little he's learned, and maybe what he thinks in his mind and feels in his heart. What use you make of it is up to you.

"When we go around towns and are among more people, as we will when you're older, you'll find there's other laws besides those you've set for yourself, but still you'll find that the best laws are those you make for yourself to follow—and a man should be strict with himself. Nevertheless, you will want to obey the laws of the towns. Folks couldn't live together unless they had respect for one another, and for the rights of other men. When you get right down to it, all law is based on respect for each other's rights.

"Now, you look at it, you'll see it takes us nearly all our time just to make a living. We hunt and we build and we mow, and we cut wood against the cold of winter, and try to salt some meat and gather some vegetables to store in the cellar.

"When folks live together in a town they have more time, time to sit and talk, to listen to music playing, or to dance. But men can't do that unless they divide the work, and in a town everybody shares. One man builds, another does the smithing, one teaches, one preaches, and another runs a store. When a man can settle down to do what he does best, he's happier, and his work is better. I guess that's where civilization began, with people getting together in a town, sharing the work, and having a chance to talk together.

"You're young, so when you sit in company, you sit quiet and listen. They say little pitchers have big ears, and they should have. That's the way to learn. You'll hear a lot of foolishness, but you'll hear wisdom, too, and you must learn not to despise any man. Even a fool can teach you not to be foolish, and there's no telling where you'll hear the thing that will help you to do a job easier, or the thing that may save your life."

When pa talked like that, Hardy just kept quiet and listened.

He remembered the time Mrs. Andy spoke to pa about him. "That's a serious-minded boy you've got there," she had said, doubtfully. "Don't he ever get a chance to play?"

Pa-had been irritated. "He gets plenty of chance. He's a thoughtful boy, and I'm glad of it. We've had a hard time here, and he's been company for me as well as a help. And there ain't a lazy bone in his body."

No use for pa to be upset; sure, he had time enough to play. There wasn't a tree within a mile he hadn't climbed or tried to climb, and he had played Indian-fighter all over the country. Only it was more fun trying to track wild game in the forest, or trying to figure out what birds and animals had been doing, by giving study to their tracks.

When pa did carpenter work on the officers' quarters at Snelling or Atkinson, Hardy had gone along. Then he had played with the youngsters at the forts; but it was more fun when he and pa were traveling through the forest, rustling their own grub. He just wished pa was here now, sitting by the fire with them.

But they were warm, sheltered, and safe for the time being. Before the snow had gotten too thick he had fixed in his mind the locations of the dead trees, and other places where he could find wood for fuel. He got up now, slipped his blanket-cape over his head, and said to Betty Sue, "I'm going to see to Red before we go to sleep." He dug into his pack and took a piece of the pilot bread, and then ducked outside.

It was snowing hard, and commencing to blow. But it was no problem to get to the stable, as he called it, for all he had to do was edge along the rock wall until it curved into the overhang.

Partly sheltered by trees and brush, it was as good a place as he could have found, and better than many a shed where animals were kept in such weather. Standing alongside Big Red, he talked to him and fed him, bit by bit, the slab of pilot bread.

"You got to help me, Red," he whispered. "I'm kind of scared, but I'd never tell Betty Sue that, because she depends on me. We must have come more'n halfway. You stay by us and we can make it."

He fed the stallion another corner of the bread, and then suddenly the stallion's head went up.

Hardy heard the sound, too. It was a wolf . . . somewhere not very far off. He let the stallion have more rope, enough so he could lie down if he was of a mind to—or fight wolves if need be. He heard

the long, lonely howl of the wolf again . . . and
then another, farther away.

Were they on their trail? Had they found the
scent of the horse and the children?

"It's all right, Red." Hardy patted the stallion's
shoulder. "It's all right, boy."

The horse nuzzled the boy, and Hardy fed him
the last of the pilot bread. With a look around,
satisfied to see that no snow had yet blown into
the shelter, Hardy went out. Snow swirled about
him, but he felt along the wall to the door, lifted
the latch, and went in. Once inside, he dropped
the bar and pulled the latch-string back through
its hole.

He added wood to the fire, and sat down beside
Betty Sue. Somewhere out in the night the wolf
howled, and Betty Sue snuggled against him.
"Don't you worry," he reassured her, "no wolf is
going to get in here."

"I hope your pa finds us," she said wistfully.

"He'll find us," Hardy said positively. "I know he
will. Why, I'd bet anything he's hunting us right
this minute!"

11

Scott Collins drew up to let the others overtake him. His face was lined and haggard, and he could see the dismay in Darrow's features. Bill Squires reined in, took out his tobacco and bit off a healthy chew, then tucked the plug away in his shirt pocket.

"Snow," Darrow said bitterly. "That was all we needed."

"What do you think, Bill?" Collins asked. "You know this country better than we do."

"She's goin' to be a storm, a real old howler. That means three, four days. We've got to hole up and set it out, boys."

The snow was thickening as they talked. A rising wind whipped the snow into their faces and flapped the brims of their hats.

"How long have we got before it's too thick for us to travel?" Scott Collins asked. "I mean if we pushed on fast?"

"Mebbe an hour, mebbe less. Look at it, Scott. If we don't find a place to hole up we're goin' to freeze to death, an' then who'll look for the youngsters?"

"All right, but let's push on as long as we can see tracks. Then we'll hunt for a place."

Squires started his pony, glancing briefly at the tracks. The tracks of the stallion were there, but the tracks of the pursuers were there too.

Intent upon the trail of the children and the two men who followed them, nobody thought to ride wide of their trail, and so those other tracks, only a little way off, went unnoticed. Ashawakie had not given up on the great red horse, and he was fully aware of the presence of Cal and Jud. With a little skill he might return with their scalps and ponies as well, and he would have much to sing about in the winter lodges.

The three men rode swiftly, all of them watching the trail, but not forgetting the country around them, either. "A man's got to be careful," Darrow said stubbornly. "This here's late for Injuns, but who knows the mind of a redskin? We're apt to come on 'em at any time."

"Pete Schifflin had him a place somewhere around here," Squires commented. "We trapped this country together, an' he claimed he found some color. All I know is that he took out of Fort Hall like the devil was after him, an' we'd only just pulled in. Slipped off by himself with quite an outfit."

"What happened?"

"He never showed up any more," Squires said. He shrugged. "Mebbe Injuns . . . who knows? A man off by himself like that . . . he might break a leg . . . or he might get down sick, an' who's to rustle grub and water for 'im?"

"It would be a good place to hole up if we could find it," Darrow suggested.

"We'd been riding the Beaver Rim," Squires went on. "We split up, figurin' to meet a few days later over at the Crow's Nest, west of here. If he found gold, it was somewhere between the Rim an' the Sweetwater."

Darrow chuckled cynically. "That's a big piece of country, Squires."

"Well, he didn't go south so far's the Sweetwater, an' we split up near the head of Crooked Creek an' I cut his trail on Beaver Creek, due west of here. We rode on up to the Nest together."

The snow was growing thicker. Now all tracks

were covered. There was no longer any question of following a trail; they could only depend on their minds.

"You're his pa—what will the boy do?" Squires asked.

"He'll do as we will. He'll find him a hole and crawl into it. We waited out storms together a couple of times up in Wisconsin. An' he'd find a place with wood an' water. That's a canny lad. My guess would be he'd found cover before he ran into the snow. He'd see it comin'."

"Which figures he'd be somewhere along a creek. He'll hold straight, unless he figures he'd do better along the Sweetwater."

"Too far."

"Yeah . . . if he knows it."

It was growing colder and the snow was thicker now. There was no longer any question of riding on. They must find their shelter quickly.

They found it on Rocky Draw, where the rock had been undercut by the creek waters. Working with axes, they soon had built a windbreak across the opening, which would also reflect their fire's heat into the overhang. There was room enough for themselves and their horses, but before they finally took shelter the ground already had a thick covering of snow.

Scott Collins dropped beside the fire, his face gray. "You were right, Frank," he said to Darrow; "they'll never make it. I was foolish to hope."

"Nothin' of the kind!" Darrow replied roughly. "You said yourself the kid was smart enough to hole up. If we were right, an' that was a grub sack he was draggin' when he left the camp of those thieves, then the youngsters have got some grub. Hell, how much does it take to feed a couple of kids that small?"

"They'll make out," Squires agreed. "The kid's canny."

Darrow went about mixing a batch of frying-pan

bread. From time to time he glanced at Collins. That's a good man, he thought, too good a man to lose a youngster like that one. He found himself trying to imagine what the boy was doing now, and he grew impatient with their own warmth, their security. Had there been tracks, he would have gone right out to look . . . but where to go? Where to look?

All through the night the snow fell, and the rising wind whipped it into drifts. Slowly the landmarks disappeared, the world became changed. The wind howled, and those lesser killers, the savage timber wolves, burrowed deep and hid to wait out the storm, some with bellies half-filled, some starving; but there would be nothing for them to eat until the storm was over. For during the storm, nothing moved but the wind . . . the wind and the snow.

The pines lowered their limbs under the weight of the snow, and a few animals sought shelter in the hollows close to the protected trunks. The wolves did not worry. They tucked their noses under the brush of their tails, curled into a ball, and went to sleep. They were used to this—it was their life.

Scott Collins was restless and irritable, but he fought down the feeling, knowing there was nothing worse in the confinement of a snowbound shelter than a man who grumbles and complains. There was nothing to be done until the storm blew itself out, and the snow ceased. To move now would mean only to waste strength in struggling against the storm.

So he forced himself to recall those times when Hardy had faced the wilderness and the cold with him, and he drew some small reassurance from the realization that Hardy would remember some of the things he had learned then.

"When the storm's over," Squires suggested. "I think we'd best waste no time, but head right on for South Pass. The boy's got to take that route, an' we stand a better chance of catchin' him that way."

Ashawakie was no longer alone. In a corner of the hills off the Flats he had come on a travois trail made by some of his people. He found them well hidden at the edge of the woods. There were a dozen warriors, seven squaws, and half a dozen children, who had made camp to sit out the storm before going on to their main camp farther to the northeast.

All through the day Ashawakie talked with them, and by next daybreak he had arranged with six warriors to accompany him to track down and attack the two parties of white men and the children. They would take their horses, weapons, and other equipment.

The two parties they were to track down were separated, and Ashawakie knew where both parties were hidden. The undertaking looked comparatively simple. There was no risk now of missing their trail. As soon as the storm ceased they would move out.

But there was one thing he did not know. Scott Collins, on the second night of the storm, had gone out again to listen into the night. He made his way up through the trees and stood there alone. The wind had died down somewhat, and he strained his ears for some sound in the darkness, not knowing exactly what he hoped to hear . . . perhaps a child's voice, crying in the night.

He had started to return to camp when he saw the tracks. Had he been less attuned to listening for every sound, looking for anything that might help them in their search, he might have missed them.

The thing he noticed first was a tree branch from which the snow had fallen or had been brushed away. All the other branches were covered with at least a couple of inches of snow . . . why not that one?

Careful to disturb nothing, he moved closer. Behind the clouds there was a moon, and the snow itself added to the light.

There were moccasin tracks in the snow, many of them, and all apparently made by the same man. An Indian had come into these bushes, had crouched here staring through the trees at their shelter. And he had been there for some time.

Scott returned to the shelter and, accompanied by Squires—for Darrow was already asleep—he returned to the spot. Together they trailed the Indian back, by his moccasin tracks, which were half filled with snow. It brought them to a sheltered spot among the trees a few hundred yards off where a horse had been tethered. Then they went back to their camp.

At daylight all three men returned and studied the tracks. "It's him all right," Squires said. "Those are the same horse tracks of the Injun who follered the kids—the one who tangled with the grizzly."

"We'd better ride loose," Darrow commented. "A man could get mighty chilly, ridin' around without his scalp in this kind of weather."

Half an hour later they cut the trail of the travois and the hunting party of Indians, heading north.

"Cheyennes," Darrow said. "He'll be meetin' up with them sure as shootin'."

They were in trouble, and they knew it. The Cheyennes might decide to ride on north—no Indian liked to fight in cold weather—but they might elect to drop back just to pick up a few scalps and ponies.

The plans of the three men to sit out the storm, which was not yet over, had gone glimmering, since their camp had been discovered. An Indian, hiding out there in the dark, could kill any man who emerged to check on the stock or to rustle

firewood. They knew they had to move on, to find
a better defensive position . . . and with luck to
come on the trail of the children.

Three miles away to the south, Cal and Jud
were holed up in an even less desirable position,
and they, too, were thinking of moving on.

Four miles down Rocky Draw, and scarcely more
than a mile from the head of Beaver Creek, were
the children and the stallion. Their tracks were now
covered with snow, for they had been the first to
seek shelter.

Scott Collins led off, riding out of the draw and
heading west. Less than an hour after cutting the
trail of the travois they were riding about half a
mile north of the dugout that sheltered Hardy and
Betty Sue.

They had no doubt their trail would be found,
and they knew there might be a fight. It all de-
pended on the Cheyennes themselves. Would they
decide to ride south on a scalp-hunting foray this
late in the season, or would they dismiss that idea
and ride on to their home?

"Scott, we hadn't better ride too far." Squires had
come up beside him. "If we get ahead of those
youngsters we'll never find 'em. If we've guessed
right an' they're holed up, they ain't likely to move
. . . an' it's startin' to snow again."

Squires's worry showed in his face. The storm
might be the end of it all. Even if the youngsters
survived it, how would they ever find their trail
again? This was a big country, and a man couldn't
hope to cover it all.

The place they found to hole up was under some
buttes that loomed above Beaver Creek. They offered protection from the north wind, as well as
from attack from that direction, and there was a
small shelter where high water on the Beaver had
stranded several dead trees upon three large boulders. These trees made a partial roof, and other
debris as well as the snow had formed the rest. It

was a place for the three men, and a combination of trees and the buttes made a rough but adequate shelter for their horses.

Scott Collins set to work to clean his guns. He had a bad feeling about the days ahead. They had been lucky so far, too lucky, he thought.

Darrow picked up some slabs of rock from the foot of the butte and placed them back of the fire to serve as a reflector that would throw the heat into the shelter. Squires patched up a few holes where the wind might blow in, covering them with pine boughs.

Collins finished cleaning his guns and then gathered evergreen boughs for their beds. After that he got together as much dead wood as he could find and stacked it at the edge of their shelter. The night was going to be a cold one, and the fire must be kept going. From time to time one of them moved out from the camp and listened. They knew there was not very much danger of an Indian attack on such a night, but it did not pay to take anything for granted.

It was still and cold when Collins went outside the camp again. A faint sifting of snow was still in the air, and his boots made a crunching sound as he went down the little slope to the creek. There was ice along the edges, but no ice in midstream. He crossed the stream on a fallen log, and climbing the bank he went up through the snow-laden trees to the slight rise beyond.

Looking back, he could see nothing of their camp. From this direction, at least, it was well hidden.

"Hardy, boy," he whispered, "where are you?"

There was no answer, no sound. The snow fell gently, silently.

12

Hardy awoke with a start. He had been sound asleep, and suddenly he was wide awake and listening. For a minute he heard nothing, then there was the sound of movement, and Big Red snorted angrily.

Hardy slipped from under the buffalo coat and tiptoed to the door. For a moment he stood there listening, and he heard a low whine of eagerness.

Peeping through a crack, he looked out. It had been snowing earlier in the night, but now it had stopped, leaving everything white and still—except for two ... three ... black spots on the snow.

Wolves ...

He could see them quite clearly. They were big wolves, and they were close by. One of them was not more than thirty feet from the dugout, and all of them were looking toward the crude stable where Big Red was. The stallion sensed their presence, and was aware of the danger.

Hardy hesitated, his heart pounding. He must try to frighten them away. Pa had told him how wolves worked. One or two of them would get at a horse's heels, staying just out of reach, but ready to run in and hamstring him if possible. Another wolf or two could circle in front, watching for a chance to rush in and grab at the animal's throat.

These were timber wolves, larger than any he had ever seen. He could shoot at them, but the derringer would be useless and the one shot would not stop them for long.

Then he thought of it . . . *fire!*

Turning quickly, he went to the fireplace and stirred the coals. Under the ashes a few were still alive, and he stirred them, adding barks and twigs that had been put aside for the purpose. He was frightened, but he knew he must help Big Red right away, before the wolves closed in on him.

He thrust a large branch into the coals and it caught fire. When it was blazing well, he took down the bar at the door and caught up the branch and rushed outside, yelling and waving the branch.

Startled, the wolves sprang away, and rushed off into the snow. Hardy went back and laid the branch at the edge of the fireplace. He glanced at Betty Sue. She was sleeping quietly, and he blessed the fact that she was tired and was a sound sleeper.

Carrying a large stick, he went out to the stallion. "It's all right, Red," he said reassuringly. He patted the big horse on the shoulder. "We'll handle them."

He stayed with the stallion a minute or two, but the chill began to strike him and he went back to the dugout and closed the door.

He dared not go to sleep again, for the wolves would be back as soon as they got over their momentary fear. He did not know how successful he would be in driving them off again, but he knew he would have to try. But first, he built up the fire.

When it was burning brightly he peered out of the door again. Sure enough, he caught a flicker of movement in the brush. One of the hungry beasts was lurking out there. What could he do?

And then a new idea came to him. Just how it suddenly became a full-fledged plan he had no idea. Twice he had gone to the door, simply opening and closing it and the sound had been enough to send a wolf loping away into the brush, but the animal had not gone far, and he had not hurried.

Outside the dugout, about halfway between the dugout and the horse's shelter, but back toward

the edge of the creek, was a big old stump. Hardy
had cut several pieces of pitch from it for kindling,
and there were droplets of pitch where it had
oozed from cracks in the old pine stump.

If he could set that afire . . .

Gathering some bark, he rubbed it to shreds between his hands, then took a branch from the fire
and went outside. He left the door open so that he
could rush in if the wolves attacked. He doubted
they would, for the man-smell was on him, and
they had learned to fear it. But he felt sure they
might soon know there was nothing to fear from
him, might realize he was small and unarmed.

On top of the splintered stump he dug out a
little hollow. It was the stump of a blow-down,
broken off jaggedly, ought to burn well. He tried
his branch, but the fire had gone out.

Going back to the dugout he got another one
from the fire, added it to the shredded bark, and
blew to tease it into a flame. It caught some bits
of pitch, which blazed up brightly.

At the base the stump was partly hollow, and
he kindled another fire there, and added fuel from
branches lying about. Soon the fire was blazing
well, and he withdrew to the dugout.

The stump was very pitchy, and pitch pine burns
with a hot, bright flame. There was a good chance
the fire would burn all night through—or through
what was left of the night.

Inside the dugout he huddled near the fire, arms
squeezing his knees for warmth, and he turned a
little from time to time when his back grew cold.

Several times he peered out, but he saw no
wolves. A long time later, when it was almost light,
he crawled under the buffalo coat and went to
sleep.

When he woke on the morning of the third day
he knew it was time to go.

The stump was burned down to almost nothing,
and the wolves might come back. They would fol-

low him, he was sure, but from a distance. Wherever he stopped, he must be sure the place was one where there would be shelter for both them and Red, and where he could keep a fire going. Wild animals were afraid of fire, and in that lay safety perhaps.

It was a gray morning, and under a sullen sky they started west once more. They had scarcely started when they came upon the travois trail of the Cheyennes, the same one Scott Collins, Squires, and Darrow had seen only a short time before.

Hardy knew a travois trail when he saw one, and a travois meant Indians. At this time of year, he thought, they were probably headed for their winter camp, so their presence in this region did not alarm him. He was more worried about the wolves, but at first he saw no sign of them.

The snow was almost eight inches deep on the level, but it was drifted in places to a depth of three or four feet. Hardy avoided the drifts, and tried to keep a straight course to the west.

Though he was scared and tired, he was glad to be moving, and the big red stallion seemed as eager as they were to be on the way. They moved forward at a steady pace, and for the most part Hardy let the horse choose his own trail.

For a while they found no tracks at all. The snow was unbroken, and there was almost no wind.

Looming close above them were the Wind River Mountains. South Pass lay to the south of the range, and it was the accepted route to the west. If all he had heard talked about on the wagon train was true, they should be at South Pass soon. He had heard them say it was mostly a big, wide-open country where a body could scarcely tell when he crossed the divide. On one side the streams flowed toward the east, on the other toward the Pacific —or at any rate in that direction. Some of the water, he'd heard them say, wound up in the bottom of the Great Basin.

The trail they were taking followed Beaver Creek more or less. Suddenly he came upon the tracks of three riders. All the horses were shod, but he could see that only in an occasional track where it had been sheltered by a tree or bush, for the rest of the tracks were almost covered by last night's snow.

"These look like yesterday's tracks," he said to Betty Sue. "It might be those men we got away from."

"There were only two of them," Betty Sue said.

"They might have picked up a friend. But no, these don't look like the same tracks. I can't make out enough to tell, though—it might even be Indians on stolen horses."

He turned Big Red away to the north, then taking a westward direction again, he followed Beaver Creek. He could not rightly see the sun, but by what he thought should be noon they had put ten or twelve miles behind them. Big Red was tireless, and they had found no place to stop.

It was midafternoon before he saw a wolf. The animal was perhaps half a mile behind them, and when Hardy turned in the saddle he glimpsed it, loping easily along through the snow, just keeping them in sight. Fear tightened his throat. If there was one wolf, there would be others.

"We've got to find a place to stop," he said. "You keep looking, Betty Sue. You might see something that I don't."

"Are there going to be wolves, Hardy?"

"Maybe. In this kind of country there generally are wolves. Nothing to worry about though," he added. "We'll have a place with a fire."

"What if the wolves come before we get the fire lit?"

"They won't come much before night," Hardy said hopefully. "We're going to make camp pretty quick."

He knew it would be no use to shoot at them.

Pa had done that once, but it only scared them for a little while, and then they had come back.

Big Red continued along Beaver Creek, and Hardy studied every nook and cranny for a place to camp. They would need something at their backs, and they would need fuel—lots of it. They also needed a place that was big enough to get the horse in with them. Twice Hardy saw a place he thought might do for camp, but each time he had to decide against it.

He kept thinking back to the tracks of those three riders. Would it have been better to have followed them? But he had no idea who they might be, or where they were going. He kept seeing tracks of animals too, for they were out and moving now, but most of the tracks were wolf tracks.

The afternoon wore on, and it grew colder. When he looked back again he saw there were two wolves now . . . and yes, another one, still farther back.

It would soon be dark. Red had slowed his pace, and Hardy knew the big horse was hungry and must be allowed to scratch away the snow to get at the grass before they tied him up. Hardy was not only frightened, but he was close to tears. There was no place to stop . . . no place. Behind him a wolf howled, answered by another. Suddenly he saw a wolf ahead of them, waiting in the trail.

Red saw it, too, but he did not turn and run . . . instead started for the animal, teeth bared.

The wolf leaped aside, in no way frightened. He was not a lone hunter, and the rest were coming. Wolves had pulled down horses before this.

Their way went down into a grove of trees, where it was dark. The stallion ran through the trees swiftly, and suddenly, in the gathering dusk, Hardy saw what he had been looking for.

Across the creek and under the shoulder of the hill was a cave. It did not look like a deep cave, just an overhang, but there was some scattered wood there, left by high water of the past.

"Over there, Red," Hardy urged, "across the creek!"

The big horse splashed through the knee-high water and up the rocky bank on the far side. The bluff rose high above them. The interior of the cave under the overhang was black and forbidding, but close to the entrance there was a small parapet of stones made for a breastwork, or for a reflector.

Hardy slid down, gathered dry sticks under the overhang, and heaped them together. From the last camp he had brought some shavings and a handful of shredded bark, and he put these on the ground under the dried sticks and started a fire. It blazed up, died down, then caught again.

Picketing Big Red on a level spot nearby, he scraped off some of the snow to get at the grass underneath, but Red needed no showing. He knew where the grass was, and went after it.

Then Hardy set to work to gather more sticks. Betty Sue came with him, walking close to him. First of all he searched for a short, strong stick for a club, and then he gathered as much wood as he could find and piled it in the hollow under the bluff. He built his fire brighter.

It would soon be night. The wolves were out there. He could already see them coming closer and slinking around. Kicking a couple of rocks loose that were partly frozen to the earth, he hurled them at the wolves—and he had a strong throwing arm. The wolves ran off a few feet, then stopped. And that was when he thought of the slingshot.

He had no rubber or anything to use for rubber, but he could make a sling. His pa had made the first one for him when he was four, after telling him the story of David and Goliath, and he had practiced with it off and on for a year. Then he discarded it until he was six, when one day he tried it again and barked a squirrel with it. After that, he had practiced a good deal. He still couldn't be sure of hitting his mark, although he did every once in a while.

With his knife he cut a strip from the worn bottom of the old buffalo coat, and made his sling. Then he hunted in the creek bottom for stones of the right size. The water was so cold that he nearly froze his hands hunting for them, but he had soon gathered fifteen or twenty.

He stood shivering over the fire, stretching his wet hands out toward the flames. . . . There was so much to do, and he was so tired. He had never been so tired in his whole life. And he was scared —scared of the wolves, of the Indians, of the cold, and of the distance to Fort Bridger.

"We're going to make it, Betty Sue," he said confidently. "I just know we are. You know that, don't you?"

"Yes."

Her voice was small, and she looked up at him, sensing something of what he felt.

"You roll up in that buffalo coat," Hardy told her. "I'll be fixing around for a while."

He took up the stick and the sling and went out to the horse. One of the wolves, a big, heavy-chested brute, was not more than fifty feet away, just sitting there. Big Red had pulled back to the end of his tether and Hardy had to go past him, toward the wolf, to pull up the picket-pin. He was afraid Red might pull away from him.

He took a step over to the horse and put a hand on his shoulder. "It's all right, Red. Don't you fuss none."

He slipped a stone into the sling and, carrying the stick in his left hand, walked toward the picket-pin. The wolf got up on all four feet and seemed to snarl, deep in his throat. Suddenly, almost of its own volition, Hardy's arm whipped over with the sling. The distance was short, and Hardy was lucky.

He heard the *thump* as the stone struck the wolf, and the animal jumped straight up, yelping in surprise and pain, and then it scrambled off into the darkness.

Almost crying with fear, Hardy tugged and pulled at the picket-pin, but it held, half frozen in the hard ground. He worked at it, and finally it came loose and he pulled it up. Then catching up the stick and the sling again, he went back toward the overhang.

He led the horse deep inside, back of the fire. There were only two pieces of the pilot bread left, but he fed Red one piece, and patted him for a time. After that he went back to the fire and heaped wood upon it.

He dragged some sticks close up to the buffalo coat, where he could just reach out from under it and put them on the fire. It was very cold. He hung up their blanket-capes so that they would not get damp, and crawled under the coat, lying on part of it, with the other part wrapped over them. He felt of the back of Betty Sue's neck. It was warm, and she was sleeping soundly.

He cuddled up, trying to stop shivering, knowing he would soon be warm. He looked out at the fire; and beyond it, in the darkness, something stirred. He reached out and put two big sticks on the fire, then pulled his hand back.

He was beginning to get warm. He knew he should put another stick on the fire, but he hated to reach out and let the cold air in. He wanted to stay just as he was, but finally he did put out his hand and add more fuel.

Then he snuggled a little deeper under the buffalo coat, warm at last. And then, not knowing just when it happened, he fell asleep.

Nearby the stallion moved restlessly, ears pricked. Slowly the wood burned down. Only ashes glowed. Beyond the fire the wolves had moved closer, just a little way out there. The big horse stamped and blew, but the boy did not stir.

A stick, propped against a stone, slid down and fell into the coals. A flame sprang up, burned brightly, then died away, and there was darkness. Only the coals glowed, and the eyes of the wolves.

13

"We should've killed that kid," Cal muttered.

Jud hunched his shoulders against the wind. The night was bitterly cold, and in the snowfall they had lost the trail. "You forgettin' that's Scott Collins' boy?"

"To hell with him!" Cal said.

They had been riding since before daybreak, and now it was long past midnight. Their horses were dead-beat and so were they. Cal, who rode bareback, had been cursing at the loss of his saddle, and neither man had seen anything remotely like the shelter they needed.

The two men had ridden out of Hangtown just ahead of a general clean-up, which had been engineered in part by Scott Collins, and in which he had taken the major role. They were just two of many who had scattered to avoid hanging, and they had ridden east with some vague idea of robbing wagon trains bound for California or Oregon.

When news of the gold strike reached the East —and it had just done so—travelers by the thousands would be coming over this road, and an organized gang could get rich quick and live off the fat of the land while doing so.

They had at first considered staying around Salt Lake, but the stories they heard of Porter Rockwell, Bill Hickman, and others of the Danites, had given them the impression it might become extremely unhealthy in that region. So their idea had been to hole up somewhere along the trail, and steal enough supplies to wait for the rush in the spring of '49.

"Hold up, Cal!" Jud pulled in his horse and sat bolt upright in the saddle. "I smell smoke."

They tested the wind, waited, and then Jud said, "Must've been mistook, but I'd have sworn—"

"I think you did," Cal interrupted. "I caught a whiff of something."

The night was still; a low wind moaned among the trees and stirred loose snow. They waited, listening, trying the wind. They smelled nothing more, and were about to go on when they heard a wolf howl.

"Ever get a close look at one of them brutes, Jud?" Cal stared off into the night. "I seen one must've weighed two hundred, if a pound. Rancher killed him over on the Green. You never seen such teeth."

Cal started on, then held up at Jud's motion "Hold on a minute," he said. "I think that wolf's found something. He don't sound like he's huntin'."

"Aw, come on! Its cold and I want to . . ."

They both caught it then, the definite smell of woodsmoke. It came from the south, and the two renegades swung their horses and walked them slowly in that direction. From time to time they continued to catch the smell of smoke.

"Somebody's got 'em a far," Jud said. "Now, Cal, don't you start nothin' with these folks. Maybe we can get a night's good sleep."

The smell of smoke was elusive—now faint, now stronger, then dissipated by the slight wind until there was no smell of it at all. For almost an hour, never more than a few hundred yards from the source, they moved up and back, working about among the trees, and finally emerging on the top of the bluff.

There the scent was strong, for they were now directly above the overhang where Hardy and Betty Sue had taken shelter.

"Look!" Jud pointed. "There's your wolves!"

At least five wolves were within sight, their dark bodies showing up clearly against the white snow. One or two moved restlessly, others just sat there, but one seemed to be creeping toward a spot right below them.

"They've spotted something down below," Jud said. "I'll lay you eight to five it's them young uns."

Skirting the cliff's edge, they found a slide that would take them to the bottom. The bluff was no more than sixty feet high, but it was sheer along most of its length, and the slide itself was steep. The horses hesitated, but urged on by their riders, they slid down in a cascade of snow and gravel.

The riders had come up with the wind in their faces, unseen and undetected by the wolves, but the nearest wolf, creeping over the snow on his belly, was close enough to rush.

The horse was trapped against the rock wall. The wolf crept a little closer, and Big Red, eyes rolling, pulled back hard on the worn picket-rope. It snapped, the wolf charged, and Hardy awoke, all in one instant.

Hardy's eyes flared opened to see the belly of the horse above him, the stallion rearing high, forefeet churning. Before his eyes the wolf suddenly charged and the horse struck hard, his hoofs missing the agile wolf by a hair as it sprang aside, but the horse was suddenly in the open, and the other wolves were charging in.

The nearest one leaped, and the stallion caught it in its powerful jaws. Red hurled the wolf to the snow, then the big horse spun, kicking and charging as the other wolves charged.

By now Hardy was up, his derringer in his hand, watching for the chance for a shot.

Then from out of the darkness came the riders. They charged in swiftly, and one of them chopped down with his six-gun. It spat fire and a wolf dropped, kicking in the bloody snow. The rider fired again, but at a fleeing target, for as suddenly as they had come, the wolves were gone.

Hardy knew the horses. Wheeling, he caught Betty Sue by the hand and darted into the darkest corner of the overhang. Running blindly, he brushed by the blanket-capes and had the presence of mind to grab them from the rock where they hung.

He had not yet explored the back of the overhang, and now he ran into a pile of stones, and scrambled over them, barking his shins and tearing his hands. Somehow he got Betty Sue over into the dark recess behind the stones, and there they crouched, shivering and terrified.

"Get a rope on that horse!" they heard Cal shout.

"I can't rope barebacked!"

"You see them young uns?"

"Damn 'em! *Git that horse!*"

Peering over the rocks, Hardy and Betty Sue saw Jud build his loop and make his cast, but as Hardy could have told him, Big Red was too canny. The horse ducked his head and ran, circled, and then came back, neck arched and head canted to one side, his teeth bared.

Jud gathered in his rope, but at that instant Red charged. He threw himself, screaming with rage, at Jud. The horse thief swung his own horse, but its hoofs skidded on the icy ground, and the horse fell hard.

Red kicked viciously, missed Jud, and then charged at Cal. Cal tried to throw his gun, but, hampered by his heavy coat, the gun did not come up fast enough. His horse reared to meet the stallion's attack, and Cal went off, falling into the snow.

Big Red's shoulder hit the smaller horse and it fell, then it sprang up and raced away into the night, the red stallion pursuing.

Cal got up, swearing and thoroughly scared. Jud was helping his own horse up. He had jumped free a split second before his pony fell, and now he was up and ready.

"Let's get out o' here!" he said. "I've had enough!"

"You can get out—I'll have that damned stallion or know the—"

He stopped and looked around. "Where are the young uns?"

"Ain't seen 'em. But they must be here."

"Fire's out," Cal said. "That ain't like that kid." He stirred the ashes with a stick. "Still some coals, but not much. I can't see that boy lettin' his fire go out on a night like this."

Cal's head turned, and his eyes swept the place. His anger made him hasty, and he overlooked both the tumbled buffalo coat and the small sack of supplies, almost empty now, that lay toward the rear. There wasn't much to see, certainly—just a few sticks of wood piled near the fire . . .

Cal looked around more carefully. "Jud, this ain't the boy's fire," he said. "That there looks like an Injun fire. Maybe those young uns never did catch that horse again. He might be trailin' 'em."

Jud considered that. Then he shook his head. "I doubt that. Without that horse those kids would never have come this far in this short a time. No, they've been here." He hesitated a moment, knowing the hair-trigger temper of his companion. "Cal, let's forget 'em and get out of here. I don't like this."

"What don't you like?" Cal almost snarled the words. "And how are we gettin' out . . . on one horse?"

For an instant Jud was silent, suddenly aware of the dangers represented by one horse between them. Of course, he might catch Cal's horse, or the horse might come back to its running mate. Otherwise they were left with one horse, and Jud had a fair idea of how long Cal would put up with that. For that matter, he had no taste for it himself.

Mentally, he stacked himself up against Cal and

did not like the result. Cal was fast . . . one of the best men with a gun he knew, and quick to shoot. Also there was that heedless cruelty about Cal, that willingness, almost eagerness to kill, with no regard for the consequences.

Jud was a bad man, and he admitted it to himself, but he was a cautious bad man, with a wholesome respect for his hide, and he had a hankering to live to an evil old age. The more he considered his future with Cal, the less likely his chances began to seem. No man in his right mind went around crossing up people like Scott Collins or Bill Squires with any anticipation for much of a future.

Collins was a law-and-order man, a quiet, hardworking man, but one who did not hesitate to stand up and be counted. His voice had the ring of authority, and Holloway had demonstrated what happened when you challenged that voice.

"No use startin' out in the dark," he said casually. "We might as well stir up the f'ar. Anyway, those young uns may be somewheres about, an' if they are that stallion will come back."

Cal simmered down slowly, complaining in his irritating nasal voice. Jud quietly ignored him, and went about getting wood without comment. Cal would settle down after a while, and he could be fairly easy to get along with when calm. The trouble was, a man had no idea when Cal would decide to come uncorked.

Then and there Jud made his resolution. He was going to get away from Cal, and at the first opportunity it seemed possible. If he ever encountered him again, he would have a plausible excuse . . . an excuse he hoped never to need.

The boy had rustled up wood and he had, as always, chosen a likely spot for his camp. Jud stirred the fire up, and after it was burning well he studied the ground for tracks. They were there, a profusion of them, but Jud's own tracks and those of the stallion had all but obliterated them.

Neither man made any move to search the back of the cave for the simple reason that they took it for granted that the children had abandoned the place some time before. In fact, there did not appear to be anything to search. The overhang was there for all to see, and the tumbled pile of rocks, the remains of an ancient wall built by bygone Indians, seemed innocent enough. Such walls are to be found in many places throughout the Southwest.

Behind the rocks, Hardy and Betty Sue huddled together. There was no way to get out, and nowhere to go if they did. Here at least there was a little warmth, for the reflector, as well as the way the air circulated, brought some heat into their corner, though not enough to keep them really warm. They needed the buffalo coat for that, and Hardy found himself looking at it longingly.

When they had scrambled to get out of the way Hardy had dragged the coat into a heap near the wall before they got untangled from it, and it lay there in the darkness now, looking almost like another rock. If he could somehow . . .

He gave up the thought even as it came to him. There was no chance. He must lie still and wait. It would soon be light, and the men might go away.

Finally both men lay down to sleep. An hour passed, then another. The sky grew pale, and Jud got up to replenish the fire. He had turned around to lie down again when he saw the coat. For a moment he just stood looking at it as if it were some strange animal, then he went over to it, picked it up, and let it fall.

"Cal," he said.

The other man's eyes opened, instantly alert at the tone of Jud's voice. "Cal," Jud said again, "there's somebody else in this. Here's his coat."

Cal sat up, staring at the buffalo coat. The coat presented a new problem, and Cal did not like problems. Moreover, ever since he first set eyes on that red stallion there had been more and more problems.

"Who'd be out this time o' year?" he asked irritably.

"Somebody's around," Jud answered. "A man just don't go off leavin' a good coat behind."

Cal stretched out again and composed himself for sleep, but the thought of the coat nagged him, and after a bit he sat up and tugged on his boots. Besides, the bacon Jud was slicing into their frying pan was beginning to sputter, and it smelled good.

"He'll have a horse," Cal commented, "and we need a horse—at least a saddle."

"He'll have a gun too," Jud warned, "and by now he must know we're here, else where is he?"

The two men ate in silence, and Hardy, crouching among the stones only a few feet away, looked down at Betty Sue and saw that she had gone to sleep again. He was frightened, for if she moved or made a sound in her sleep they would be discovered at once, and Hardy had no doubt what that would mean.

He lay there, clutching the derringer with its single bullet, and there was no doubt in his mind as to what he must do. No matter which one discovered them, it was Cal he must shoot. Cal was the meanest one, and it looked to Hardy as if even Jud was afraid of Cal.

But he really didn't want to shoot anyone. All he wanted was to find pa, or some nice folks somewhere.

Only a few miles to the north, Ashawakie, leading his small band of six Cheyennes, started the ponies through the snow and headed south. They expected to be gone from their camp for only two suns, and to return with both ponies and the loot from two camps. Ashawakie had put in his claim for the red stallion beforehand.

In the meantime, in the cold of early dawn, Scott Collins gathered wood for their fire, then climbed atop the highest ground and stood staring around. The clouds had disappeared, the air was clear, but it was intensely cold.

His eyes swept all the vast space, lying white and still, and he saw nothing, no movement anywhere, and he heard no sound.

He could not ask Darrow and Squires to stay out any longer. No youngsters could live through this weather, and if they fell in the snow it might be spring before their bodies could be found. But though he could not hold the others any longer, he had no thought of giving up himself. Hardy was his son, and Betty Sue was the daughter of his friend.

He turned to start back to camp, his boots crunching on the snow.

It was then he saw the smoke.

14

The smoke was far off, and was not much more than a suggestion in the sky, not to be recognized except by eyes accustomed to all the shadings and changes of mountain, plain, and sky. The quality of the eyesight is often of less importance than the selectivity of the brain behind the eyes. From the hundreds of patterns and the shadow-play of sunlight and storm, the conditioned eye is quick to choose that which is different, or seems different.

Just as the eye of the trained tracker can see a disturbance in the dust invisible to the casual eye, so anything that does not fit, that does not belong, is quickly seen by the man trained to the wilderness.

What Scott Collins saw was a vagueness in outline only a shade different from the trees around, and above it a scarcely perceptible shading against the sky. Under other circumstances it might be dust or it might be smoke, but with snow on the ground dust was eliminated, and he was sure it must be smoke.

But he did not move to call the others. It was all too easy to lose such a sight, to return to what seemed the same position but was off just enough to make the smoke invisible. He remained where he was, and with great care he chose landmarks, lining up a route that would take him to the smoke. Only when he was sure of its location did he go back to the camp.

Squires and Darrow listened, then Squires got

up and set about smothering the fire. "I think it's worth a look," he said.

Within minutes they were moving out, holding to the cover of trees, emerging only long enough to check their direction. All three rode loose in the saddle, with their rifles across their saddles. The smoke might mean the children were there, but it also might mean either the Indians or the horse thieves.

"That rider now," Darrow said suddenly, "I recall who it was."

They waited.

"It was Cal Thorpe. Least, that's the name I knew him by. A bad actor, that one."

"I know him," Squires said. "He's killed a few men. They suspicioned him of robbing sluices around the Dry Diggin's." He looked over at Scott Collins. "That's what they called Hangtown afore your time. In the first few weeks they called her that, and Cal was around then. There was a lot of us down from Sutter's place to the Dry Diggin's together . . . Cal was in the outfit. He's a mean one, all right . . . quick as a snake an' just as untrustworthy."

The country over which they had to ride was rough, and there was no direct route. Time and again they had to swing wide to avoid some obstacle, but always they found their way back to the course Scott had chosen. At times they spread out, searching for tracks, but they saw none until they were in an area they believed to be close to where the smoke had come from.

Frank Darrow threw up his hand suddenly and motioned them over. "Indians," he said, "at least four. Mebbe twice that many."

It would complicate things. They had no desire to run into a bunch of scalp-hunters. They wanted only to find the missing children, not to have a fight with Cheyennes. Besides, a lot of shooting might draw more Indians down on them—the Sioux traveled this country, too.

"Headed southeast," said Squires. "D'you think they saw that smoke?"

"Mebbe. Could be that Injun who was follerin' the kids took off to line up some help, seein' our tracks like he did. We're goin' to have to ride careful."

Scott Collins would not allow himself to hope. He realized that the fire might not mean the children at all. It might be from some other passing travelers or hunters. Not that travelers were apt to be in the area at this time of the year. Nobody in his right mind would want to be out in the open.

Whatever smoke there had been was gone now. They knew they were within a mile or perhaps less of the place the smoke had come from, but their landmarks, taken from a distance, could give them no closer clue to the actual spot.

"We could scatter out," Darrow suggested.

"No." Scott was definite. "There's too much risk. We'll stay together and throw a loop around the area, cutting for sign. Anybody who rode in here should have left some tracks, and if we ride a circle we'll sure enough find them."

"It'll take us a while," Squires said, "but it's better than goin' it blind."

They rode with caution. Scott Collins took the lead, guiding his horse among the trees until they reached the fairly open boulder- and brush-strewn area beyond. The only tracks they found in the snow were those of coyotes and rabbits. Coming down a slope, they watered the horses at the Little Beaver.

It was very cold and still. The air was crystal clear, and they listened, sensing the wind for any slightest sound.

"I don't like it," Squires said in a low voice. "She's too quiet. We know there's Injuns about."

Scott led the way across the stream and up the bank beyond.

Under the overhang, Cal finished the last of the bacon in the skillet. "I got to get me a horse," he said. "I don't cotton to this place."

"It oughtn't to be hard to catch that pony of yours," Jud said. "I should saddle up and have a look around."

He held his breath, waiting for Cal's reply, but Cal was thinking his own thoughts. "We could head back for Californy," he was saying. "I've heard that Pueblo de los Angeles is a live place. An' it's warmer than here."

"All right," Jud said, "I'll go hunt up your horse."

Cal looked up, his snake-like eyes followed Jud as he picked up his saddle. "All right, Jud," he said, "You find him. But you be almighty sure you come back. If you don't, I'll track you to hell an' gone, but I'll have your scalp."

"Don't talk foolish. No man in his right mind would want to ride alone through the country between here an' the coast. You set tight . . . I'll find that horse."

He gathered the reins and put his foot in the stirrup with the hair prickling on the back of his neck. Not for a minute did he believe Cal would let him ride away—yet he did. He simply sat there watching as Jud moved off slowly.

Immediately Jud was out of sight Cal got up, and he was grinning. "You damn fool," he said aloud, "don't you suppose I know whose coat that is?"

The story of Pete Schifflins's gold was widely told in the cantinas of California, and Cal heard it there. Moreover, he had known Pete, and had even seen a sample of the gold. Not many believed in the story and quite a few did not know gold from iron pyrites, but Cal did. He had been one of those who helped push the Cherokees off their land in

Georgia because of the gold strike there, but that had been piddling compared to California.

He had recognized Schifflin's coat the instant Jud held it up, for Pete Schifflin had one short arm, caused by a bad break years before, and he had hacked off the end of the sleeve to allow free use of his hand.

If that was Schifflin's coat, then somewhere around had been Schifflin's diggings, and that probably meant a cache of gold.

He got up and went to the far end of the overhang, and with quick, practiced skill he began scanning the wall, the ground, the whole layout. If there was a cache here, there would be some sign of it.

Hardy lay still, listening. He could not see Cal from where he lay, but the man was busy doing something near the end of the overhang. Hardy desperately wanted to peep out, but he was afraid of being seen. He could hear Cal coming nearer, but so slowly that Hardy could not guess what he might be doing.

Then Cal came within sight. Hardy saw him examining the rock wall, moving rocks that lay against it, obviously searching for something. When only a few feet from the rocks that hid them, he turned and went back to the fire, replenished it, and stood there warming his cold fingers. Then he poured a cup of coffee and started to sip it.

Hardy was shaking with cold, and his fingers were stiff. He tried to cover Betty Sue a little better, but he was fearful that he might wake her. He even thought of trying to run for it, but Betty Sue could not run fast enough, and he was afraid Cal would shoot them. Touchy as he was, he would be likely to shoot at anything that moved . . . and he had intended to kill them, anyway.

Cal sipped his coffee slowly. Close beside Hardy, Betty Sue was waking up. Her eyes opened, and Hardy put his finger over his lips. He looked long-

ingly toward the trees and brush, not over twenty
feet away. He could see the body of the wolf Cal
had killed lying out on the snow, and a thick clump
of trees just beyond it.

All of a sudden he had an idea. He put a stone in
his sling, drew his arm back, hesitated, then threw
it hard toward the brush beyond the wolf. It struck
the trunk of a tree there with a loud crack, and
Cal threw himself sidewise, grabbing for his gun as
he moved.

Hardy had never seen a man move so fast. Nor
did Cal stop; he changed position swiftly, moving
out to a pile of rock, and retrieving his rifle as he
did so. There he lay, poised and ready to shoot,
leaving Hardy no better off.

If they tried to move now, the slightest noise
would make Cal turn around, and he would turn
shooting. Hardy had hoped to get him out into
the brush, away from the cave. He fitted another
stone into the sling. There was only just enough
room to throw if he threw flat, with a side-arm
swing.

He pitched the stone, getting this one farther
out. It lit in the brush and Cal's rifle muzzle lifted
slightly, but he remained where he was, obviously
puzzled. Then he got up to his knee, ready to
move.

"You get ready," Hardy whispered. "We've got to
run."

Cal moved so swiftly they were caught napping.
He lunged into the brush and was gone, like a
shadow. Hardy and Betty Sue moved only an instant afterward, into the brush on the other side,
and once there, they crouched under a bush.

Cal was gone for some time while they huddled
there, not daring to move, scarcely daring to
breathe. Then they saw him come walking back,
taking his time, not even looking around until he
was close to the fire. He turned his head, and suddenly froze.

Hardy looked where Cal was looking, and was appalled. There were their tracks, clear and fresh in the snow. Where they had crossed to get into the brush the snow had been untouched by man or beast, but now their tracks were plain to see.

Cal strolled over, studying them. Then he looked toward the brush and spoke casually. "You young uns might as well come in. She's almighty cold out. You'll surely freeze."

"Hardy, let's go back to the fire. Please." Betty Sue didn't know the trouble that lay in that man yonder.

He dearly wanted to be warm himself. It was colder than it had ever been, and their coat was back there. Maybe they could somehow . . .

"Come on in where it's warm," Cal said, his voice mild. "We got things to talk over, boy. You an' me, we might make ourselves a deal." Then he added, "I know where your pa is."

Was the man lying? Hardy hesitated. Betty Sue tugged at him, and reluctantly he got up. "Will you take us to pa?" he asked.

"Sure enough," Cal said. "You tell me where the man is who left that coat, an' I'll take you to your pa."

They could at least get warm. If they tried to get away now, he could track them anyway. It was best to go in and try to win him over. Hardy wasn't very confident of that, but the idea of the fire was too much for him. "We're coming in," he said.

They walked in, hand in hand, and Cal squatted by the fire, staring at them through his small, cruel eyes, smiling a little. "Want some coffee, boy? You an' that gal best have some. It warms you a mite."

When Betty Sue was sipping coffee, and trading sips with Hardy, Cal asked, "What about the man who wears that coat, boy? Where is he?"

"I don't rightly know."

"You know when he'll be back?"

"No, sir."

Cal's irritation showed. "Now look here, boy. Don't lie to me! That coat's been wore, recent."

"We've been sleeping in it. We brought it here."

"You're lyin' like hell. You didn't have no coat before."

"No, sir. We found it."

He stared at them suspiciously. "Found it? War?"

"Back yonder. We camped in a dugout during the storm. The coat was there. So were the kettle and the frying pan."

Cal thought about that and decided it was probably true. Pete Schifflin was a canny man, and this was not a likely place for such a man to hole up.

"You didn't see anything of that man Schifflin?"

"We didn't see anybody. The coat was all dusty, and it hung in a sort of closet. Nobody had been around that dugout in a long time. That man must've gone off and maybe hurt himself somehow. Or Indians got him."

"Why do you say that?"

"Well, nobody had been in there. The coat was hung out of the way, so I figure it was hung up during some time when he didn't have any reason to wear it. I don't think he went away to stay, because he left too much of his outfit behind."

Cal considered this idea, and accepted it. "You're a right smart boy," he said. He filled the cup again for them. "Now, if Jud comes back, you're not to say anything about this, d'you hear?"

"I won't if you give me some of whatever it is you're after," Hardy said.

Cal chuckled; he seemed pleased. "You'll do, boy. You'll do. What do you figure it was Schifflin had?"

"Gold or furs," Hardy said; "and I don't think it was furs. I didn't see any traps around there, nor any cache either. I think it was gold."

Cal studied him, interested in the boy in spite of himself. He was a shrewd man, who was filled with hatred for anything or anyone that opposed him in any way, but he appreciated cunning, and he felt that the boy had it. It would be a shame to kill him. If it wasn't for that baby . . .

"You see any of that gold?" he asked Hardy.

"No, sir, but I figure a body could find it. I don't figure he'd want to travel much for fear of being seen by Indians. The more he moved and the more tracks he made, the better their chance of catching him. So I figure that gold was somewhere close by the dugout."

"Good figurin', boy. You got any other ideas?"

"Yes, sir. I think that man went off and got hurt. I didn't see any shovel or pick around, nor an axe either. So I think he had them with him when he was hurt, or maybe killed . . . or he left them at the diggings. I think that's what he'd do. He wouldn't want to have to fetch them back and forth every day, because he'd want to carry his rifle to use if Indians came."

Cal seemed to be thinking the matter over, while Hardy edged closer to the fire. He still had the derringer. If Cal tried to hurt Betty Sue he would shoot him.

All the time Hardy was thinking hard, wondering what they could do to escape. If they could get away, he desperately wanted to take the coat with him, and some food.

It was good to be warmer now, but he did not like the way Cal kept smiling at him. Hardy had been talking more than he usually did, trying to gain a little time.

He had seen greedy men before, had seen his father bargain with them, had seen the look in their eyes, as he could see it now in Cal's eyes. But he saw something else too, something that frightened him, and he knew they must escape or be killed.

"You young uns jes' take it easy," Cal said calmly. "I figure we got us a chance to git rich, but don't you say a word if Jud comes back. That

Jud, he's a mighty mean man, an' he don't cotton to youngsters."

He smoked thoughtfully for a few minutes, and then said, very casually, "You figure that horse of yours is somewhere about?"

"He might be. I don't think he'd go far."

"S'pose you called him an' he heard you . . . would he come?"

"I think so," was the quiet answer.

"Now, s'pose you walk up yonder on the rise there. You just go up there an' call out a few times. I'd say maybe eight or ten times, with a little wait between. I'll jes' keep your li'l sister here with me . . . sort of to make sure you'll come back."

"Don't you hurt her," Hardy said.

"Now, boy, what kind of talk is that? We're pards, ain't we? Anyway, you know where that Schifflin dugout is, an' I don't, so I ain't likely to get you sore at me, boy. You git up there now an' call out."

Hardy walked away reluctantly. Slowly he started up the rise. It was less than seventy long paces from where Cal sat, and would be an easy rifle shot. And Cal was holding Betty Sue.

On the climb to the top, Hardy could think of nothing he could do. He was getting chilled again, and he was hungry and tired. He felt weaker than he had at any time before. But the worst of it was not knowing what to do, and he felt so alone. He cried a little as he climbed the hill.

Standing up there, he looked back. Cal was sitting with his rifle in his hand, and Betty Sue was on the ground near the fire, where he could see her without really taking his eyes off Hardy.

The top of the hill was bare. Beyond it were low-growing trees and some brush and rocks, but he could not see far because there were thicker trees farther along.

He called out, "Red! Red!" He waited to let the

echo die, and then called again. "Red! Red! . . .
Come!"

The air was very clear, and even his small voice
carried well. He waited again, looking up at the
sweeping rise of the Wind River Mountains, only
a few miles off to the north. Then he called once
more, directing his voice toward the mountains.

Scott Collins, turned his horse away from the
bluff above Beaver Creek and started north, Bill
Squires and Frank Darrow trailing behind. They
had lost any trace of the smoke, though they were
now within a few hundred yards of it; and the
wind, little as there was, carried the smell off to
the south, away from them.

Scott turned in his saddle. "Damn it, Bill, I—"

He did not complete the sentence. Faint, yet
not very far off, they heard the call: "Red! Red!
. . . *Come!*"

15

Scott Collins started to cry out when a hard hand grasped his arm. "Scott!" Squires's voice was hoarse. "Ssh!"

He pointed. . . . On the slope opposite, perhaps a half-mile away, three Indians rode, one behind the other. Three of them . . . and then another, and another.

"We'd better get down there fast," Darrow said. "They've heard that boy, too. And they're closer'n we are, I'm bettin'."

The bluff was steep, and was littered with gigantic boulders, thick brush, and stunted trees. They rode swiftly along the rim, looking for a way down. It was Squires who led the way now, for he had covered this rim before. Soon they found a way down, steep but negotiable, and they slid their horses to the bottom.

From the knoll where he was calling to the stallion, Hardy could see the opposite slope, and he glimpsed an Indian an instant before the men on the rim did. He turned and ran down the slope, back to the camp.

Cal got up and spoke angrily. "You git right back up there an' call that horse!" he yelled. "Damn you, if you—" He pointed the pistol barrel toward Betty Sue.

Hardy stood there. "You'd better listen, mister! There's Indians coming!"

"You're a-lyin'," Cal said, but he was suddenly

139

wary. The boy did not look as if he was lying, and he was frightened, downright scared.

"How many did you see?" Cal asked.

"There's five or six . . . maybe more. I didn't wait to see. There was an Indian that followed us, and there was travois sign back yonder. He could have rounded up a mess of them to come after us."

Cal swore viciously. No chance to get away . . . *and where in God's world was Jud?*

"Come on, boy. We'd better hole up an' lie quiet."

He swiftly went back to the cave and looked around. It could be worse. There was the partial wall of rocks somebody had thrown up for defense or for a fire reflector, and there was the corner behind the rocks where the children had hidden.

The very fact that he had no horse might help. It was just possible that when the Indians discovered that they would leave him alone, deciding the fight wouldn't be worth what they would get out of it.

"Get down behind those rocks in the corner," Cal told the children, "an' stay out of sight."

Pulling all his gear in behind the wall, Cal hunkered down there. He had a little food and over a hundred rounds of ammunition. The field of fire was a pretty good one, but if those Injuns were smart and started shooting at the back wall of the cave he was finished. The ricocheting bullets could tear him into chopped meat—he had seen that happen before now. But most Indians lacked enough experience with firearms to do that; and not even many white men were likely to think of it.

Behind the rock pile where the children lay close together, Hardy could see very little. It was darker back where they were, and he thought that the Indians might not even see them.

"Don't be scared," he whispered to Betty Sue. "We'll be all right."

"I wish your pa would come."

"He'll come—you'll see. You can just bet he's comin'."

But how could pa ever find them now, hidden as they were? Maybe he was still waiting at Bridger. After all, the wagon train couldn't have reached there yet, even if it had kept going. Or maybe it would have just about been there by now. Hardy had lost track of the time.

He could feel Betty Sue trembling. He wondered how much she had guessed about her ma and pa. She never talked of them any more, and he did not mention them, for he did not want her to think about them. Sooner or later she would have to know, but he hoped that wouldn't be until both of them were safe in a warm place with pa to watch over them.

Betty Sue was so thin, and her eyes always had a frightened look in them now. As far as that went, he must look a sight himself. His hands were thin and his wrists were skinny; his ribs stood out from the flesh.

Cal spoke softly to them: "You be quiet now."

Hardy could see him lying there with his rifle ready, and a neat double row of ammunition laid out on a flat rock in front of him. He had a breech-loading percussion carbine manufactured by Jenks. It was a .52 caliber, and was a good shooting gun.

For a long time there was no sound, and Hardy's breathing got almost back to normal. He was even hoping Betty Sue would go to sleep, but she was wide-eyed and listening, just as he was.

Suddenly Hardy thought of the bodies at the wagon train. How still they had been! How tumbled and strange-looking! He felt his throat grow tight, and he was trembling. Betty Sue touched his hand. "Hardy, are you cold?" she asked. "You're shivering."

He put his head down on the rocks and struggled to hold himself still. "Yes, I'm cold, " he answered. "I wish we were closer to that fire."

Cal was lifting his rifle, very slowly. Looking in the direction the rifle pointed, Hardy saw not even the faintest stirring of leaves.

Everything was quiet. Not a sound stirred the morning. The air was still . . . and how cold it was!

Then the stillness was shattered by a weird cacophony of yells, and from the brush tumbled the body of a man. He was on his knees, and for an instant it seemed as if the man would stand up and walk, and then he toppled slowly forward and rolled over.

It was Jud.

Hardy heard a choking ugly sound from Cal, then there was silence. Taunting yells came from the woods, trying to draw his fire. Suddenly a rider burst from the trees and went sweeping by. As he passed the overhang he let fly with an arrow, which smacked harmlessly into the wall shielding the fire. Cal did not shoot.

Several minutes passed, and then another rider came from the opposite direction, lying far over on the side of his horse. He let go with another arrow. Still Cal did not shoot, but just as the horse turned up the slope toward the trees the Indian's back was momentarily revealed, and Cal fired.

Hardy was looking at the Indian and he saw his body wince, but he was still clinging to his mount when he disappeared into the trees.

A volley of bullets spattered and ricocheted among the rocks, the booming thunder of their reports reverberating from the cliff. One bullet struck a rock in front of Hardy and scattered stinging fragments all around. Betty Sue tightened her body close to him and whimpered.

"It's all right," Hardy said to her. "Those ol' bullets can't get to us back here."

He said it only to ease her fears, for he knew that, though they were out of the line of fire directed at Cal, a ricochet might hit them.

Cal, evil though he might be was no fool. He did not waste a shot holding his fire for the right target. In case of need, he had his pistol as back-up.

After the crashing thunder of the volley it was silent. Cal kept turning his head to right or left, watching for some try at taking him on the flank. That he was frightened was obvious, and it was with reason. He was fighting alone, and he had no horse. Jud was out there, dead. If Cal came out of this alive, he was going to have to do it alone.

Hardy knew the Indians could not see into the darkness behind the pile of rocks, and he peered out, trying to see if there was any way of slipping into the brush without being seen. The trouble was, he did not know where all the Indians were.

He could guess what Cal was afraid of. If the Indians rushed him from several directions at once, he might get one, even two or three of them, but they would surely get him. He might get one with his first shot with the rifle, but he would have no chance to reload, and must draw and fire his pistol. He would be very lucky, considering the few yards the Indians had to cross, to kill even one with the pistol.

Hardy's heart was pounding hard. He stopped looking out and buried his face against his arm to shut out the scene before him. He tried to think . . . but what could he do? He had done all he could, but it simply was not enough.

Then he remembered something he had heard. When an enemy is struck down, all the Indians try to get in a blow, to count coups on the enemy's body. If Cal was downed, wouldn't they all close in around him, crowding close to strike at the body? Mightn't there be a chance just at that moment? . . . Or would it be better just to lie still here and hope the Indians would not find them?

The silence and waiting continued. Hardy looked out again, watching the brush for some movement, but he could detect none. He saw some low evergreens out there that had sprung up after an old fire, most of them two to four feet high. Trees were back of them, and there was more brush. He thought he saw, off to the left where the trees grew close together, the shadow of something moving.

He stared hard, and something moved again—it was something large, and seemed to be of a dull copper hue. . . . It was Red!

In that light, the coat of the horse looked duller . . . but of course, he was putting on his winter coat. . . . But Red was there, close by!

A surge of excitement swept through Hardy. He almost rose up in his wild eagerness to run to the horse, to throw his arms about him. For a moment he scarcely thought of what the Indians might do to him, but even as he seemed about to call out, he stopped. The Indians would never let such a horse escape them, and they would kill Hardy or capture him, and Betty Sue as well.

However, the very sight of the horse, the knowledge that he was near, gave him hope. He didn't know how it could be done, but there must be some way of getting to Big Red. And once on the back of that stallion, nothing in this country could catch them.

"Boy," Cal said softly, only for Hardy's ears, "that horse of yours is out there. You call him now. Call him in."

"I won't."

"Boy"—Cal spoke quite calmly—"those Injuns ain't apt to kill anybody as young as you. I want a runnin' chance. Now you call that horse, or I'll kill the both of you. I'll do it myself, without waitin' for no Indians."

At this moment there was room for only one

thought in Hardy's mind. Big Red, in the hands of such a man? Big Red, who had always trusted Hardy and loved him.

"No," he said. "I won't do it."

"One more chance," Cal said. In his voice the thin line of sanity that stretched between Cal's calmness and his insane fury was almost broken. "One more chance, boy. I'll kill the girl first."

He half turned, rolling on his shoulder a little, to lift his pistol. "You got mighty little time, boy, an' that girl's got none at all. You call him now. I seen him out there, so call him."

Cal eared back the hammer on the pistol, and the click was loud in the silence.

16

Hardy was sure that Cal meant to do just what he said, but there was no panic in him now. The hunger and the cold, the constant fear, the nights of worry and the days of struggle had given him something strong, even when they had been making him grow tired and weak. He was thinking now, and he knew that Cal would have to shift position to get a shot at them . . . or wait until the Indians had gone, if they ever did go.

"Mister"—Hardy's voice was low, but it carried far enough—"you stick your head out to get a shot at me, and one of those Indians will sure enough kill you."

"Boy," came Cal's wheedling tone, "you toll that horse over here. On him we can all git away . . . scotfree!"

Now that was a sure enough lie. If the horse came close, one man might jump on him and ride off . . . he just might . . . but the odds were against it. But three people? And the time they would take mounting up? There would be no chance of it, and Cal knew it. Cal wanted Big Red for himself, and if he did throw himself into the saddle and get away alive he would have Big Red to keep—and Cal was a mean, cruel man.

"No."

"Boy"—Cal's voice was trembling with fury—"I'm tellin' you! I'll kill—"

Two guns fired almost as one. In twisting about, Cal's boot had thrust beyond the rock, and the two bullets spat sand, one of them doing no more than that, the other ripping the heel from his boot.

Cal jerked his foot back, and swore with deep and awful fury. Turning, he fired with his rifle into the brush where the shots had come from, then swiftly reloaded.

Hardy was almost afraid to look for Big Red; how long would it be before the Indians discovered him?

"Betty Sue, you be ready now," he said. "We may have to run real fast . . . all of a sudden."

"All right."

At the end of the overhang just beyond where Hardy and Betty Sue were hidden behind the rocks, the space between the roof and the rock floor was only about four feet. Elsewhere along the front of the cliff the roof was six or seven feet above the floor. The rocks that now formed the pile had once been a wall enclosing this recess, which might have been a storage place for grain, or perhaps merely a sleeping shelter.

Peering out under the overhang towards the woods where Big Red stood, Hardy looked fearfully at the open stretch that separated them from the trees. It was possible they might get into the trees without being seen, but the chance was slight. Clinging to Betty Sue's hand, he edged that way, keeping well down behind the rocks.

Another shot came from the Indians. Apparently they were undecided about attacking. To attack meant a warrior would die, and no Indian wanted to face certain death. To do a daring deed that he could sing about in the winter lodges was one thing; but this was something different.

Ashawakie knew they could kill this man—it was only a matter of time. He advised patience, so they waited.

But Ashawakie was restless, for it irritated him that the big red horse was not here, as he had believed he would be. They had captured two

horses and they had taken a scalp. They had a
rifle, a pistol, some clothes, and a blanket, along
with a few odds and ends. Their foray was not unsuccessful thus far, but to Ashawakie it would be a
failure if he did not get the great red stallion.

Cal spoke again. "Boy, you got one more chance.
I tell you, no matter what happens, you call that
horse or I'll shoot the both of you!"

Hardy did not reply. He had just seen an Indian coming down from the brush on the far side,
creeping closer and closer. If that Indian was seen
by Cal, Cal would shoot, and they would all be
looking. . . .

The Indian was well around on the right side
of Cal, and close enough to make the try. He sprang
up and, knife in hand, he charged.

Instantly Cal wheeled and fired, and as he did
so Hardy grabbed Betty Sue's wrist and they
darted out from under the end of the overhang
and ran for the woods.

Cal's rifle shot caught the Indian full in the
chest, at almost point-blank range, and the sound
of the blast was still in the air when Cal wheeled,
pistol in hand, and fired into the woods. And then
he saw the children.

With a hoarse shout, he swung all the way
around to fire, but at that instant there was a
burst of firing from the woods. Cal held his fire, for
the shooting was not directed at him.

An Indian burst from the woods, lying low across
his pony, plunged across the open space, and was
gone before Cal could do more than snap a quick
shot that missed. From other parts of the woods
dashed several others; one shot at him, the others
fired behind them at some unseen enemy.

In an instant they were gone. The crash of gun-
fire ended, the Indians had fled. In the stillness
there was the acrid smell of gun powder.

"Red!"

Cal turned sharply as the boy called. The stallion burst from the brush, whinnied softly, and came quickly up to the boy, who stood waiting, holding the girl by the hand.

The ugly fury, throttled by his inability to move while the Indians kept him under fire, burst now in a sudden, unreasoning desire to kill.

"Boy, bring me that horse!" The gun was up, tilted in his hand, ready to fire.

Hardy turned around, standing stiff and straight. "You leave us alone!" he said. "And you leave Red alone!"

The gun started to level in a coolly deliberate plan to murder, when Scott Collins stepped out from the trees.

"Drop it!" His voice rang sharply. "Drop it, Cal!"

Cal went to one knee behind the rocks and fired as his knee hit the ground. He aimed not at the children, but at Scott Collins.

Scott's rifle muzzle had been lowered, but it came up in one easy move just a little above the hip.

Cal saw the leap of flame just as his own finger closed on the trigger. He felt the thud of a bullet on his chest and started to stand up for a better shot. The second shot, aimed at his head, caught him in the throat as he lunged up. The pistol dropped from his fingers and he fell, hit the rock parapet, and toppled over.

He rolled free, muttered a curse and tried to push himself up, then fell back.

Hardy was staring at his father. "Pa?" His voice was a trembling sound. "Pa ?"

Scott went to him and dropped on one knee. "Hardy . . . Hardy, boy . . ." His voice was low and hoarse, and it faded out. He could not speak, but he caught the boy to him and clung to him, looking beyond him at Betty Sue.

"Come on, honey," he said to her, and gathered her to him.

Fifty yards away, Bill Squires drew up alongside Frank Darrow. Squires took his chewing tobacco out, looked at it speculatively, then bit off a small piece. "You know something, Frank?" he said. "To be honest, I never thought we'd find them."

"You didn't?" Darrow grinned at him. "I reckon I always did, Bill. I figured if the boy was anything like his pa he would just keep a-comin', and he done it."

Scott Collins got to his feet. "Come on," he said, and he gathered the reins of the big horse. "Climb up, Hardy. We've got to be moving on."

When the boy was in the saddle, he lifted Betty Sue up.

"Pa," Hardy said, "there's a buffalo coat yonder. We carried it off from a dugout a ways back. Can we keep it, pa?"

"You'll need it. We've got a cold ride."

He walked over to the coat, glancing only once at Cal. He remembered him now from Hangtown— he had known him the instant he put eyes on him.

When he was again in the saddle, and Hardy was wrapped in the buffalo coat, the boy said, "Pa? You carry Betty Sue. I think she'd like it."

"I'd like it, too, Hardy. I surely would," Scott Collins said.

The snow crunched under their horses' hoofs, and a slight wind stirred, sifting a little loose snow. Some of the snow settled in the creases of Cal's clothing, along the line of his lips, upon his open eyes. The wind stirred again, and more snow sifted down.

Hardy hunched his small shoulders under the buffalo coat, warm and snug. Somewhere ahead was Fort Bridger, and pa was riding right behind him.

ABOUT THE AUTHOR

LOUIS L'AMOUR, born Louis Dearborn L'Amour, is of French-Irish descent. Although Mr. L'Amour claims his writing began as a "spur-of-the-moment thing," prompted by friends who relished his verbal tales of the West, he comes by his talent honestly. A frontiersman by heritage (his grandfather was scalped by the Sioux), and a universal man by experience, Louis L'Amour lives the life of his fictional hero. Since leaving his native Jamestown, North Dakota, at the age of fifteen, he's been a longshoreman, lumberjack, elephant handler, hay shocker, flume builder, fruit picker, and an officer on tank destroyers during World War II. And he's written four hundred short stories and over eighty books (including a volume of poetry).

Mr. L'Amour has lectured widely, traveled the West thoroughly, studied archaeology, compiled biographies of over one thousand Western gunfighters, and read prodigiously (his library holds more than twenty thousand volumes). And he's watched thirty-one of his westerns as movies. He's circled the world on a freighter, mined in the West, sailed a dhow on the Red Sea, been shipwrecked in the West Indies, and has been stranded in the Mojave Desert. He's won fifty-one of fifty-nine fights as a professional boxer and pinch-hit for Dorothy Kilgallen when she was on vacation from her column. Since 1816, thirty-three members of his family have been writers. And, he says, "I could sit in the middle of Sunset Boulevard and write with my typewriter on my knees; temperamental I am not."

Mr. L'Amour is re-creating an 1865 Western town, christened Shalaka, where the borders of Utah, Arizona, New Mexico, and Colorado meet. Historically authentic from whistle to well, when it is constructed, it will be a live, operating town as well as a movie location and tourist attraction.

Mr. L'Amour now lives in Los Angeles with his wife Kathy and their two children, Beau and Angelique.